LIFE
on
REPEAT

AMY LARSON MARBLE

HILDEBRAND BOOKS

Nashville, Tennessee

Hildebrand Books is an imprint of W. Brand Publishing.

j.brand@wbrandpub.com

www.wbrandpub.com

Printed and bound in the United States of America.

Cover design by designchik.net

Publisher's Note: This is a work of fiction. Names, characters, places, and incidents are a product of the author's imagination. Locales and public names are sometimes used for atmospheric purposes. Any resemblance to actual people, living or dead, or to businesses, companies, events, institutions, or locales is completely coincidental.

Life on Repeat / Amy Larson Marble—1st edition

Paperback ISBN 978-1-950385-15-7

eBook ISBN: 978-1-950385-16-4

Kindle

Library of Congress Number: 2019918246

CONTENTS

"No sound, once made, is ever truly lost.
In electric clouds, all are safely trapped,
and with a touch, if we find them, we can
recapture those echoes of sad, forgotten wars,
long summers, and sweet autumns."

–Ray Bradbury, *Now and Forever*

How would you live your life if you knew it wasn't your only one? Would you do anything differently if you knew you would have to do it all again? I'm not sure how many lives I have lived, I only know this is not my first—or my second. I don't know if I'm the only person living one life after another—it could be happening to everyone, and they just don't remember. I remember. But as far as I can tell, I'm the only one. My name is Sarah Daley and I'm 19 years old. . .again.

CHAPTER 1

THE MOMENT

The *"moment,"* as I've come to call it, is when the memories of a past life break through the surface. The first *moment* I remember clearly happened when I turned 14 years old. In that life, my name was Sarah Mackenzie, and I was a ninth-grade student in Mount Washington, New Hampshire. I wasn't the prettiest girl in the school, or the most outgoing, but I had a few close friends, and for the most part was content in my life. My parents were still married, but I wouldn't have called it a happy marriage. My mom was into new age discovery and "finding herself." My dad called her a hippie, and mostly ignored her and her quest for self-realization. First it was the sweat lodge, followed by the meditation retreat, and floatation therapy after that. He didn't ask her to stop, so I guess he was supportive of her in his own way.

That morning started out no different from any other. I woke to my alarm and hit the snooze button—twice. I ignored my mom as she yelled from the bottom of the stairs for me to get up, followed by a much louder yell from my dad telling me to listen to my mother and get out of bed. I begrudgingly flung my blankets aside, put on my fuzzy pink slippers, and trudged down the hall to the bathroom to take a shower. Showers in our house had to be either short or cold. My dad had been working on the pipes to improve the water pressure, but like most of his do-it-yourself projects, it would only be a matter of time before my mom would convince him to hire someone to do it.

After a slightly too long and unpleasantly chilly shower, I went back to my room to find something to wear. I looked in the mirror and frowned at my reflection. I wished I had the color of my mother's dark blonde hair rather than mine, which was best described as somewhere between mousy brown and the color of dirt. My mom's blonde came from a box now that she had begun to get the occasional gray hair, but it was still beautiful. I took too long deciding what to wear and ran out of time, so I settled on a tie-dye T-shirt, jeans, and my boring brown hair tied up in a ponytail. I ran downstairs to the kitchen, inhaled a frozen waffle, washed it down with a glass of orange juice, and ran out the door to catch the school bus. As usual, I almost missed it, but my best friend Jan waited for me and begged the driver to hold the bus while I sprinted to the corner. Jan was a free spirit. We were such opposites. She was fearless, while I was not. How we ended up best friends was a mystery to me. She would walk straight up to a boy she liked and tell him he should ask her to the school dance.

"It's 1974, Sarah. You don't have to wait for the boy to ask you. This is the age of enlightenment," she would say. "You have to seize the moment, or it will pass you by."

Jan and I had homeroom and fourth period algebra together. Algebra was not Jan's favorite class, but I, on the other hand, was more comfortable with numbers than I was with people. On weekends I would help her with her math homework, and she would help me with pretty much everything else, like what clothes to wear to the movies, or what to say to the cute guy in my science class the next time he asked to borrow a pencil.

That day was normal until my class with Jan. We walked into algebra and sat down at our assigned desks. Mr. Gramm seated us alphabetically, so Jan was right behind me. Class began and we were told to open our books to page 48. Just then, Jan poked me in the back. I turned around with a furrowed brow on my face, thinking she was going to start whispering in class again. I hated getting in trouble in front of all the other students. It never seemed to bother her, but I found it absolutely humiliating. Jan leaned toward me.

"Are you okay? You look kind of pale. Did you skip breakfast again?"

"No, I'm fine. I ate. I'm probably just tired. I had a hard time sleeping last night. It was as if I was dreaming with my eyes wide open."

"Quiet down girls," Mr. Gramm warned. I turned back around quickly, knowing that I was the one who kept talking this time, so I couldn't be upset with Jan. Not that I ever really got upset with her. If anything, I wished I could be more like her.

I listened to Mr. Gramm explain today's lesson while trying to avoid eye contact as he looked for volunteers to come to the front of the classroom. I knew the answer to the equation he had hastily written on the chalkboard, but I hated talking in front of the whole class. I scribbled busily in my notebook, grimacing so it would look like I was having trouble working out the equation. That's when it started. I looked at my paper, and instead of numbers, I had been writing names. I looked at the page again. "Jenny," "Thomas," and "Andrew" were scrawled in big bold letters. Stranger still, I didn't know a Jenny, Thomas, or Andrew. There was a girl named Jennifer in my science class, and I had once met a Thomas at a church potluck, but I didn't have friends with those names. Mr. Gramm's first name may have been Andrew, but there was no reason that I would be writing those names, over and over, on my homework assignment. It was odd, but I assumed I was so bored that my mind was wandering. I'd always been easily distracted, so it wasn't surprising that my thoughts would drift. Algebra ended, and we filed out into the hallway to go to our next class.

Fifth hour was gym. I despised that class. I changed into my gym uniform, which consisted of a boxy grey shirt with a pair of black shorts that hung past my knees. I had forgotten all about the names written in my notebook, because God help me, we were playing dodgeball. Dodgeball was probably the most sadistic game ever created. The entire point of the game was to throw a hard rubber ball with as much force as possible at another human being. I could see the value of this if one was training as a gladiator, but for a ninth-grade girl with poor coordination, I always felt more like a target than a gladiator.

I didn't put much effort, if any, into trying to grab a ball to throw at the opposing side. If I couldn't get an ice cube from the freezer without it slipping through my hands and dropping on to the floor *every single time*, how was I supposed to accurately throw anything while trying to avoid inbound rubber missiles? It seemed unlikely. Instead, I cowered in the back as much as I could, and tried to hide behind braver souls than I. Just as the girl in front of me was tagged, I heard a voice from behind me. I turned around, but no one was there. . .just balls bouncing off the wall behind me. I shrugged my shoulders, and

6

then *whap!* It was a direct hit. The hard ball smacked me right on the side of my head, knocking me down to the hard wood floor of the gym. My ears were ringing, but I quickly stood back up, more embarrassed than injured. Then I heard the voice again. The gym teacher blew her whistle, she yelled something at the boy who launched the missile at my head, and I heard it again. . .someone right behind me. This time, it wasn't spoken like someone talking to me, it was more like laughing. It was a girl's laughter, but when I turned again, there was still no one there. I was thoroughly confused and wondered if maybe the ball had hit me harder than I realized. The gym teacher, Miss Deacon, asked me if I needed to go see the nurse. I jumped at the opportunity to escape the brutal dodgeball assault and went to lie down in the nurse's office.

Nurse Susan was waiting for me, having received a call from Miss Deacon that I would be arriving soon. She pointed to the back room and told me to rest while she went for a new ice pack. I laid down on the only cot in the office. It was covered with a pale blue sheet that matched the color of the walls. The office reeked of rubbing alcohol and antiseptic. It seemed more pungent than usual, and I had to pull my shirt up over my nose to block out the smell. I closed my eyes and started to think about the voices I had heard in the gym. I couldn't place them, but there was something familiar about them. It was like when you see a movie or watch a commercial, and you know you've heard the voice before, but just can't place the name. It was starting to eat away at me. The nurse came back from the supply closet with an ice pack for my head. It didn't really hurt anymore, but I didn't want to chance being sent back as a dodgeball target, so I accepted the cold ice pack with a weak smile and uttered a more pained than necessary "thank you" to the nurse. I placed the pack on the side of my head, then *Bam!* It felt like another dodge ball had hit my head. Images started rushing through my mind. . .there was a girl with short dark brown hair and blue eyes, laughing. She stood by a locker in a hallway and was laughing at something a boy had just said. It was Jenny. I didn't know how I knew her name was Jenny, but I was sure of it. Then the boy walked up closer to her. He was taller than Jenny, and his light brown hair kept getting in his eyes as he talked to her. He reached across to give a soft shove to Jenny's shoulder. I could feel his hand. But I was in the nurse's office. Jenny laughed again and told him he should tell that joke to Andrew. It was like I was watching a movie, but it felt as real as if I were standing there with the two of them in the hallway. *What hallway? Where?* I wondered. I was in a hallway with Jenny and Tommy. But I was in the nurse's office. *Who were Jenny and Tommy?* My heart pounded in my chest. My head started to spin, and I thought I might throw up. I called out to the nurse, telling her that I was going to be sick. She ran back to me with a bucket and told me to roll onto my side. She pulled my hair back from my face, and asked if I would be okay while she called my parents to come pick me up.

"I'll be fine. Thanks." This time I didn't need to fake the pained sound of my reply.

My house was only a couple of miles from the school, so it was less than 10 minutes before my mom arrived to take me home.

"Oh Sarah, sweetheart! Are you okay? Do you think we need to go to the doctor?" My mom was a fervent believer in frequent visits to the doctor. Very frequent. "Better safe than sorry," she would say. She would say that a lot.

"No, Mom. I just want to go home and rest."

"Are you sure? You could have a concussion. I think I'd better at least call Dr. Kevin."

"No Mom, please," I pleaded. "I really just want to go home. I feel a little better already." Mostly I just didn't want to see "Dr. Kevin." His real name was Dr. Kevin McDonnally, but he thought he was more relatable as "Dr. Kevin." Considering he was like, 100 years old and smelled far too much of off-brand aftershave, it would take more than a nickname to make any kid relate to him. Besides, what could I have told him? That I was hearing voices and seeing people and places in my head? He'd call in the brain trauma specialists as fast as his century-old fingers could dial. I spent 10 more minutes convincing my mom that I was feeling much better, and she reluctantly agreed to take me home.

"I won't be able to stay with you. I have an appointment, but I'll call you every 15 minutes to make sure you're okay."

"Really, it's okay Mom. I'll be fine. You go to your appointment. Really, I'm fine."

When we pulled up to our house, my mom walked me up to my room to make sure I wouldn't faint, have a seizure, or any other variety of medical emergency before she would finally leave for her appointment. She tucked me in bed, fluffed my pillows and pulled down the window shades.

"Stay in bed. I got the long extension cord, so I am putting the phone right by you. Call the doctor's office if you need me, otherwise I'll be back in two hours. Are you sure you'll be okay here alone?"

"Mom, really, I'll be fine. It was just a rubber ball. I probably just have a stomach bug. I'm feeling better already. Really, go."

I heard her go downstairs, rummage in the kitchen drawer for her keys, and then shut the door behind her. It was all of two seconds before I jumped out of the bed and grabbed a pen and paper. I needed to write down everything swimming around in my head if I was going to make any sense out of it. I started writing the names again.

Jenny
Tommy
Andrew
Caribou High School

Caribou High School? I wasn't sure where that came from. I had never heard of it. I grabbed the atlas from my desk and started paging through the index. It took me a few minutes just to find it. Caribou, Maine, page 48, section C10. I flipped open the book to page 48 and looked at the map. Sure enough, there it was. Caribou, Maine. I'd never been to Maine, and yet, I knew the color of the walls in the high school hallway. I knew my locker number was #172 and inside it was a small mirror with a hot pink frame. The mirror was a gift from my mother on my first day of freshman year. . . Jenny's freshman year. I knew Tommy's locker was down the hall to the left from mine, and Andrew's locker was #173, right next to mine. As sure as I was that I was Sarah Mackenzie, and that I was in my bedroom in Mount Washington, New Hampshire, I also knew that I was Jenny. Or that I had been Jenny. My head started to spin again, and this time I did get sick.

I climbed into bed and somehow managed to fall asleep. When I woke up, it was early evening. I stared at the clock in disbelief. I hardly ever napped, much less for hours. I was exhausted. Exhausted from the thoughts running through my mind. I had lived a life before this one. A gate to my past had opened, or a wall had come down, or a veil lifted... it didn't matter how I phrased it, because there was no stopping it. The images grew stronger with even greater clarity and more detail. I wasn't hallucinating or dreaming. I was remembering. I was remembering my life, but not this life. Not my life now. Tommy had been my best friend, and Andrew was the cute boy with the dimples whose locker was next to mine in the hallway. I had known each of them and could see their faces and hear their voices as clearly as if they were standing beside me that moment. My name had been Jenny Ames and I was an 18-year-old girl in my senior year at Caribou High School in Caribou, Maine. I wanted to know more. I needed to know more about my life as Jenny Ames, but I wasn't sure where to start. My mom and dad were both home at the time. It would have been difficult to explain a trip to the library after the visit to the nurse's office. The research on Jenny Ames would have to wait. I planned to use my Saturday to look for anything I could find about her. My mom called upstairs to me, asking if I wanted anything to eat.

"No thanks Mom. I'm still kind of queasy. I think I'll just wait until morning." I didn't want to risk seeing her or my dad at that moment; surely, they would have been able to see that something was different about me. I dropped back down in my bed, my head spinning and my heart pounding. Even so, I was asleep again within a few minutes. I dreamt of a blue-eyed boy with brown hair that fell across his forehead. The girl in my dream arranged her locker and placed the hot pink magnetic mirror on the inside of the door, hoping it wouldn't break if she shut it too hard. She waited by her locker for a boy with dimples, hoping he would ask her to the school dance. When I woke, it was late in the evening. The dream stayed with me, each detail like the stars shining outside my bedroom window, right there, but still just out of reach. I walked out to the front porch to put my thoughts together, and sat in the swinging chair my dad put up for my mom's birthday. She loved that swing. It didn't seem like a gift she would enjoy, but she loved it. I guess my dad knew her better than I thought. I sat down on the swinging chair and tried to clear my head. I stared up at the night sky, and the stars shone with a brilliance unlike any

I had ever seen before. The darkest parts of the night sky were a deeper black; undulating, almost liquid. I kept staring at the stars until my eyes lost focus and the entire sky was one swirling wave of dark and light. I breathed in the night air, and I could hear her voice. It sounded almost like mine, just slightly lower. Jenny's voice. I saw her clearly then. She looked like me, but had shorter hair and blue eyes. She and Tommy had been best friends since kindergarten, and he pretended not to know that Jenny had a crush on him. It felt as real to me as the swinging chair on our front porch. I wanted to tell someone, but I needed to know more first. I knew it would sound crazy, but this was huge. I knew—or at least hoped—I wasn't crazy, but I didn't know who I could trust with something like this. It would need to be someone with a very open mind. I thought about maybe telling my mom. She had always professed a desire to expand her mind and broaden her horizons, and this news definitely fell into that category. As I rocked on the swinging porch chair, I drifted off to sleep a third time. It was well into the night before I woke again. I went inside, snuck upstairs to avoid scaring my parents, and made plans for my trip to the library. I needed to figure out where I could find out more about Jenny Ames. The morning came fast, and I snuck out before breakfast so I could be there when it opened.

I loved the library. The musty smell of old books, and the quiet calm that came with a space where silence was required. The orderly stacks of books placed neatly on towering shelves. The huge wooden staircase with a railing that I always wanted to slide down, but never did. I came here whenever my mom and I fought—which was often—and it always helped me find some peace. Everything made sense here until now. Nothing made sense anymore. Nothing would until I figured out how I had been Jenny Ames.

I started with the bits of information I managed to piece together from the visions of my life as Jenny. I knew she was a high school student in Caribou, Maine, so I started there. I asked the reference librarian if they had any high school yearbooks from Maine, but that was a dead end. Then it occurred to me there was another possible record of the life of Jenny Ames. . . her death. I looked up the obituaries from the Caribou Gazette, starting with the year 1950. I wasn't sure when Jenny had lived, but I had to start somewhere. In some of my visions, she wore a skirt with ankle socks, so it was a worth a shot. I asked the librarian again for her help, and she set me up with a drawer of microfiche slides. The only way I was going to find out anything was to search through hundreds of slides, but I didn't know where else I could get information on a girl hundreds of miles away, and from years ago. It took me a few minutes to load the machine, even though the librarian had just shown me how to do it. I figured out which number slide of each publication held the obituaries, and soon I was scrolling through the films at a feverish pace. I had been going through the slides so quickly I almost missed it, but then there it was.

> Sarah Jennifer Ames, *'Jenny'* to her friends and family, beloved daughter and sister, passed on Monday, May 18, 1959. She died from injuries sustained in an automobile crash and is survived by her parents, Michael and Sara Ames, and her sister, Susan Ames.
>
> Sarah Jennifer will be laid to rest in Downy Meadows Cemetery on Saturday, May 22nd following a service at Our Mother of Grace Church.

Reading it took my breath away, but it was the photo underneath that hit me like a punch to the gut. It was the last photo ever taken of Sarah Jennifer Ames.

It was me.

The grainy, black-and-white photo was of *me*. The hair was darker, and much shorter, but there was no mistaking it. . .it was me. I had been Jenny Ames, and now I had proof. I don't recall going home, only that by the time I arrived, I resolved to tell my mom everything. I would wait until the morning, because I was still too anxious after the day's revelation to attempt a conversation of that magnitude. As I lay in bed drifting in and out of sleep, I dreamt of Jenny.

The next morning, I woke ready to share my discovery with my mom. I started down the stairs but chickened out almost immediately. Thinking I could muster up my courage in the shower, I walked back upstairs, into the bathroom, and turned on the water. I slowly took off my pajamas, hoping the extra time would heat up the water before I got in. I found my favorite terry cloth robe—a bit tattered around the bottom, but still very cozy—and hung it on the ceramic hook next to the shower. I stepped into the streaming water, and despite the ample warm-up time, the temperature hovered at lukewarm. My plan for a long shower—or to be more precise, my stalling tactic—was failing miserably. I showered quickly, and grabbed my robe to dry off. I wrapped a towel around my head, looking for comfort in my normal post-shower routine. Even as I tucked the towel in behind the nape of my neck, I knew nothing was going to be normal about this day.

I started down the stairs again, and heard my mom and dad discussing their upcoming appointments of the day. My mom needed her dry cleaning picked up, and my dad agreed to get it on his way home from golfing, and asked if she would swing by the pharmacy for him before her acupuncture appointment. She sighed, as if it was a huge inconvenience, but agreed. I continued down the stairs, hoping my dad would leave before I hit the last stair. I knew I would not have the courage to tell him as well, and I wanted to get this over with as soon as I could. I peeked around the corner. My mom was looking in a small mirror, frowning as she analyzed the fine lines that had started to form around her eyes. She spent a lot of time and money on products designed to maintain her youthful appearance. "There's nothing wrong with giving nature a little help, Sarah," she always said when I commented on her vast array of skin creams and wrinkle serums. She peered into the small mirror and barely noticed as my father kissed her on the cheek and walked out the side door to his car. I waited for the sound of him driving away before I approached her. She looked surprised to see me up, at least without her having to call me down for breakfast two or three times.

"Hey, Mom. What's up?"

"Good morning sweetheart. You're up early. Did you sleep well?"

"Uh, fine, thanks. Um, okay, I guess. Well, not really." It was not the most eloquent start.

"Something on your mind, sweetie? You look troubled."

Apparently, I didn't hide my emotions well. I took a deep breath, and said "Yeah. I have to tell you something." The color drained from her face almost instantly, perhaps a natural reaction of any parent when their teenage daughter makes such an announcement.

"Mom, I have lived another life. Before this one. Like. . .as another person." I realized at this point that all hope for eloquence was long gone, so I continued as best I could.

I told her about the images, the voices, and the details of my former life as Jenny Ames of Caribou, Maine. Her face paled further, looking more like a white sheet than her usual tanned and glowing complexion which she worked so hard to maintain.

The words weren't out of my mouth for more than two seconds before I wished I could have swallowed them back up. At first, she stared at me, as if she was trying to decide if I was joking.

"That's not funny, Sarah. Why are you doing this? You know I have a busy schedule. I can't be bothered with your bizarre idea of a practical joke today."

"I know it's not funny, Mom. It's not meant to be."

She stared at me for what felt like hours before jumping to her next conclusion.

"What are you on? Is it pot? Whatever drugs you're taking, we can help you Sarah. I know the best doctors. We'll help you beat it."

"Mom, I'm not doing drugs. I don't get high. I swear. I'm trying to tell you something, and I need you to listen with an open mind."

My plea for understanding fell on deaf ears. I guess I understood. It was a lot to swallow. In my mom's mind, the only possibilities were I was either on drugs or I had suffered a mental breakdown. Without another word to me, she went to the telephone and called her therapist for a referral. After a few miserable days of telling and retelling my story to Dr. Keller, a heavy-set balding man in an ill-fitted suit, he and my mom had me placed in a "safe environment" where I could talk about my *feelings*. I spent the next two years in and out of psychiatric wards, psychiatrist's offices, and healing facilities. I learned quickly that sharing the *moment* with anyone was not a wise idea. My final escape from the Sunny Meadows Healing Center came in the form of an overdose of sedatives, accidently administered by a new nurse on staff. My life as Sarah Mackenzie ended at 16 years old, alone, in a room with white walls.

CHAPTER 2

APPEARANCES

I don't know how many times someone has walked up to me and told me how much I resembled someone they knew. It has happened a lot. An elderly woman named Esther told me I reminded her of a high school friend. An older gentleman at a restaurant mistook me for the girl who used to live next door when he was a boy, but "Oh, that was way before your time, but what a resemblance." Sometimes I remembered them and the lives where we met. Esther had been my classmate in high school. We often sat at the same table in the school cafeteria during lunch. I remembered how she would complain how all the food on our trays tasted the same, whether it was some unidentifiable meat-like product or the watered-down mashed potatoes. That had been in Caribou, Maine.

As my memories returned, I noticed a disturbing trend. In all my past lives, I had yet to live past 23. I didn't know if it was a cosmic thing, or if I just had incredibly bad luck, but since I don't believe in luck, I would have to say the universe hated me. Sometimes I didn't even make it past my teens, but to date, 23 was my record. It doesn't bother me as much anymore. I used to freak out about it, cowering at each birthday, convinced that each milestone hurled me ever closer to yet another untimely death. Occasionally I found myself wondering how death would happen. Perhaps another car accident, or maybe an allergic reaction to a bee sting. I hoped it would not require another long stay in the hospital, only to still die anyway. I remember the faces of the hospital staff when they told me there was nothing more they could do. They all marveled at how well I took the news. A death sentence was easier to take when you were certain you'd live again.

I kept a journal of my lives, more of a catalogue really. It helped me organize the sequence of my existence so far, although I think I've lived more lives than I have been able to list. Some of the memories were from times and places that didn't fit within the lifetimes I could clearly recall. The timeline got fuzzy before I was born as Jenny Ames in Caribou, Maine. Perhaps my memories from my life as Jenny would eventually fade if I kept coming back again and again. Sometimes in the visions, I was dressed in clothes more fitting to the 1800's, but I couldn't get a clear picture. It was like something from a dream: The harder I try to recall it, the faster it disappeared. All that was left was the feeling of yet another lifetime. There were times I found I knew how to do things, things I shouldn't have known how to do, or didn't recall learning. For example, I'm an excellent downhill skier even though I've never taken lessons, at least not as Sarah Daley. I have a working knowledge of first aid and can knit with my eyes closed. It's hard to explain, but when the situation presents itself, I often find that I can do things I didn't know I could. Things that I've never done before in this life come as naturally as if I'd mastered them, which somewhere in some lifetime I must have, and it stuck with me. I think maybe it's a muscle memory of the psyche. Sarah Mackenzie's mom would have liked that one. She was an avid enthusiast for all things mystic. Yet with all these skills of unknown origin, I still couldn't swim. Multiple lives and I still haven't learned to swim. Maybe I could knit a life preserver.

CHAPTER 3

MINNEAPOLIS/SARAH KENT

In my last life, my life as Sarah Kent, the *moment* came when I turned 16. It wasn't as hard to accept that time. The clarity and understanding of my unique existence came more quickly and allowed me to move on with my current life as best I could. Although I had come to accept my seemingly unending existence, it was still unsettling. I felt as though I was stuck in syndication; a living, breathing rerun of a formerly lived life.

I lived in Minneapolis, Minnesota. Why I was always born in some freezing cold part of the world, I had yet to understand. Maybe there was something to the whole karma thing, and I was paying for misdeeds in a past life by having to endure seemingly endless winters. Despite freezing days and bitter cold nights, my life as Sarah Kent was uneventful and for that, I was grateful. I'd had my fill of drama.

I never embraced new age philosophies, and would roll my eyes at healing crystals, aromatherapy, or any therapy for that matter. It was likely a residual effect from my years of therapy in my life as Sarah Mackenzie. Certainly, that had not ended well. It wasn't until my life as Sarah Kent, on the day of my 18th birthday, I decided to do some research to find out what was happening to me. I went to the library at the University of Minnesota in search of answers. Walter Library was deep in the heart of the campus, and always a long, cold walk from the nearest bus stop. I walked in, still shivering from the piercing cold that was a part of life in Minnesota at least six months of the year. The huge front door creaked as if the hinges would snap at any second. I began with the premise that what was happening to me may be reincarnation, and checked out every book I could find on the subject. After hours of research, I didn't feel any closer to an answer than when I first walked through the doors of the musty old building. The university's library didn't have much of a selection, so I asked the librarian if he could help me. He suggested I try a store called The Book House. A short five-minute bus ride later, I found myself at the corner of 4th Street and 13th Avenue in Dinkytown.

As soon as I walked in, the door chimes caught the attention of the store clerk. She was a middle-aged woman with untamed, curly gray hair, the kind that went in every direction. She wore a tie dye dress that belonged more at Woodstock in summertime than Minneapolis in mid-February. She saw me and called me over to her.

"You've been searching, haven't you dear?" Her voice was soft and melodic. When she spoke to me, it reminded me of the way a mother speaks to her frightened toddler.

"Excuse me?" I replied, not sure what she meant, and distracted by the strong scent of jasmine in her perfume. She placed her warm, soft hands on either side of my face. She wore large chunky rings on each of her fingers, even her thumbs.

"You, my darling, are an old soul. But one without a true sense of who you are. You are searching. I can help you." Perhaps she wasn't as out there as she first appeared.

"Actually, I would really love that," I replied, finding myself close to tears.

She led me to the back corner of the store. A large sign that read "Spirituality" hung over the dark wooden shelves. She showed me several books on reincarnation. I bought a few, took the long bus ride home, and waited until I was in the privacy of my room before I even took them out of the bag.

I spent the next six days reading. Each book was essentially a variation on the same theme. If I understood correctly, the reason I kept coming back life after life was because I was a mess, and I would continue coming back until I wasn't a total screw up. It was not the answer I hoped for. One of the authors, a Buddhist priest who was called "The Wise Yogananda," wrote that souls could be held back not only by their own Karma, but that of other souls as well. If I got my act together enough to end the roller coaster of my existence, I could still end up with another repeat because of some other screwed up soul. *Really* not the answer I hoped for.

Another theme among the books was the grouping of souls. The premise was that each soul played out several different roles, whether as a mother, father, or daughter, that enabled it to relate to others from different perspectives. All souls continued to be drawn to each other, life after life, but their relationship was different with each incarnation. My father in this lifetime could be my cousin in the next, or I would be the father the next time around. In theory, my existence was proof of reincarnation, but there was one problem, one glaring, huge difference. I was always *me*. I had a different name, but essentially, I was still *me*. Each life had different counterparts, and yet, I had always been myself. The color of my eyes or hair might have changed, but my features, my face and build, were always the same. That didn't fit with any book or research. My search for clarity was at a dead end. Finally, exhausted and no closer to an answer, I resigned myself to my fate. Whatever I was going through, I was doing it alone. If there was some grand design in this, I'd failed to grasp it. Maybe I was on the forefront of a new kind of reincarnation; the evolution of reincarnation. Or maybe there was no great design or plan. What possible reason could there have been to keep skipping me through time, one short life after another? Some people wake up after a good night's sleep and briefly wonder what day it is. . . for me, it's what decade.

With my research having left me with little to show, I went about my everyday life as 18-year-old Sarah Kent. I was busy with school and had a part time job at the public library, so the days passed by quickly and without much variation. I didn't mind the repetition of it all. It was comforting, and gave me a sense of continuity. My parents, Bill and Sherry Kent, tried their best, but dependability was not their strong point. Blended with my own special brand of neurosis, it wasn't difficult to understand how familiarity comforted me. Then one unusually warm day in May of 1996, I met someone. He was unlike anyone I'd ever met before. I met Luke.

We met at a street dance in a small neighboring town. It only had a population of 800, but would swell to over 4,000 on the night of the annual street dance. I was at the event with my best friend, Pam. It had not been our original plan for that evening; in fact, we made a point of avoiding it.

"It's nothing but a bunch of drunken cowboys with overly ambitious hands." Pam said. I agreed with her, and we planned for a quiet girls' night at home. Chick flicks and popcorn with extra butter, but air-popped to avoid the extra calories. The air-popping was pointless, but it made us feel better. We had rented *Say Anything* for the fifth time. I was melting the butter in the microwave when I heard Pam call out from the other room.

"This will be way more fun than the street dance. There probably won't be any cute guys there anyway, right?"

"Right. Absolutely. Probably not a single guy worth meeting. Just a bunch of drunken cowboys," I called back to her from the kitchen.

I had overheated the butter for the popcorn, and it was bubbling as I took the hot bowl out of the microwave. I burned myself on the rim of the bowl, yet somehow managed to not drop the entire contents, and set it safely on the counter. I wasn't completely unscathed. My quest for buttery popcorn had left me with a large red burn mark on my palm, just below my thumb. It throbbed as I ran it under cold water. *That's going to leave a mark*, I thought. I grabbed a towel from the side of the kitchen sink and used it to grab the bowl of melted butter. I poured it over the popcorn, doing my best to distribute it equally.

There's nothing worse than soggy popcorn. Pam's kitchen smelled like a movie theater as the butter dripped over the popped kernels. This had been the right choice. A quiet girls' night at home.

"Get dressed. Let's go." Pam stood in the kitchen doorway. She had her purse in one hand and coat in the other.

"What? But what about the movie?" I asked, "and Lloyd standing underneath Diane's window playing their song? I want to see them fly away together."

"We've seen that movie so many times, Sarah. I know the street dance will probably be lame, but what if my soul mate is there and meets someone else while I'm watching John Cusack hold a boom box over his head? Could you really sleep at night knowing *my* soul mate is married to someone *else*?"

"No, I suppose not. I'll get dressed."

We climbed into Pam's Honda Civic and after two lollipops and a 30-minute drive, we arrived at the street dance. I always had lollipops on hand, much to the dismay of both my mother and dentist. I stood firm in my belief that lollipops could make almost any situation better. Before getting out of the car, Pam accidentally sprayed on too much perfume with some of it landing on me in the process. It smelled like lilacs and baby powder. I hated the smell of lilacs—of most flowers really—and the smell of baby powder reminded me of changing a diaper. That's not the image I wanted to pop into a guy's head if he was close enough to smell my perfume. Pam talked during the entire drive, so I was anxious to get out of the car. Not that I didn't enjoy talking with Pam, she was my best friend. I just didn't enjoy the topic. *Soul mates.* Pam was a fervent believer in the idea that one perfect person was out there for each of us, and fate would ultimately bring these soul mates together. Apparently, she didn't trust fate to take care of all the details, given the fact we drove more than 30 miles to a street dance at 11:30 at night, just to make sure her soul mate didn't end up with someone else. I had a hard time with the whole idea of soul mates. One person out there for me—one person out of billions—the odds seemed impossible. I was too practical to believe in soul mates. If my succession of lives had taught me anything, it was that the universe was a random, chaotic place. The idea of soul mates finding each other in that environment was almost comical. Pam, on the other hand, was a hopeless romantic. Even her last name, Hadley, meant "field of lavender," which I would admit was a romantic setting. Smelly, but romantic.

The street dance was in full swing when we arrived, and all the parking lots were full. We had to drive 12 blocks away to find a spot, so I was grateful that my boots were not only cute, but comfortable too. I would often sacrifice comfort for style. The boots were short with taupe suede with fringe running down the back. If I had believed in luck, I would have called them my lucky boots. I checked my hair in the rearview mirror before I got out of Pam's car.

"Pam, do you have any hairspray with you?"

"Here," she replied, handing me a huge Aqua Net can from her purse. After applying a couple of coats of hairspray that smelled like lighter fluid or some other highly flammable liquid, I gave up on my hair looking anything other than straight and limp and handed the large spray can back to Pam.

"Thanks. Do I look okay?"

"Beautiful, darling. The boys won't be able to resist you."

"Now I remember why you're my best friend. Even if the dance is lame, I'm glad we got to hang out tonight."

"Me too. Now, let's move it."

We quickly covered the 12 blocks to the dance, and paid for our admission bracelets, which were the same blaze orange used by hunters during deer season. It wasn't great for color coordinating with an outfit, but at least we all were in the same boat. We went inside the sawhorse barricades that blocked off the dirt street, which was a makeshift dance floor. The band played country music, and except for a few older couples who knew how to dance to it, the street was filled with high school and college students, flailing around as they attempted some version of the Two-Step. The guys spun the girls around, and the girls would squeal as they twirled and stumbled without direction. I watched the dance floor thinking, *I gave up Lloyd and Diane for this?*

Pam called to me. "Sarah, come here. I want you to meet someone." She was fast. We'd only been at the dance for 10 minutes, and she was already talking to a tall guy with brown hair. He was wearing a sweatshirt from the University of Minnesota. From the look of him, he was probably a freshman, possibly a sophomore. I walked over to them. "This is Tim. Tim, this is my best friend, Sarah."

"Nice to meet you," he said.

"Yeah, you too," I answered. I looked at Pam while Tim glanced away, asking her with my gaze if she was trying to set me up with Tim or if she was interested and was seeking my approval. She mouthed, "My soul mate." That answered that. I gave her another look, which gave her the approval she sought. Tim was cute, pleasant enough, and it wasn't like he was down on one knee asking Pam to marry him, and I needed to disapprove. There would be plenty of time for that later.

Pam giggled at everything Tim said, and frequently flipped her hair to the side as she talked with him. It was entertaining to watch, even if it had the potential to be a train wreck. Pam's heart had been broken more than once. For me that was yet another valid reason to *not* believe in soul mates. Tim must have noticed me staring blankly as I pondered the theory, patting myself on the back that I wasn't easily taken in by such notions.

"Hey, Sarah, that's your name, right? I've got a character for you to meet."

I didn't say anything but smiled weakly. *Great,* I thought to myself. *I could have been eating soggy buttered popcorn in my comfy jammies, but no, I'm here, listening to a band play country music, and badly at that. By all means, bring on the character.* "Hey Luke, come here. I want you to meet someone." Tim called to a boy who was about 10 feet away. He walked over to us, and suddenly I was glad I wasn't eating soggy popcorn in my comfy jammies, and the music didn't seem so bad.

Luke walked over to us, and smiled as he approached. His smile was disarming and mischievous at the same time. His dark blonde hair whipped around in the wind that had picked up just in time for our arrival and was laying waste to my recently applied layer of hairspray. Luke said "hello" to Pam, and then looked at me. He stared at me for a moment before saying anything, as if he were studying my face.

"Have we met before?" he asked. I was disappointed a bit by the obvious pick-up line, and replied "That's a good one. . . did you come up with it all by yourself?" I had said it more harshly than I intended and wished I could take it back as soon as I did. Fortunately, Luke was not swayed by my reply.

"No, really. . . you look so familiar," he persisted.

I was grateful for the second chance at our first meeting, and I played along.

"Where do you live?" I asked.

"I live in Saint Paul, and I go to the U of M." It was the start of a conversation that would continue on through the night. It was 6:00 in the morning before Luke asked if he could kiss me, and when he did, I knew I would have to reconsider my theory on soul mates.

CHAPTER 4

LUKE

It was the morning after the street dance, and Luke and I had spent the entire night talking. After a long walk past a horse barn and down to the lake, we went back to Pam's place and watched the sun come up over the water.

"Have you ever been horseback riding?" he asked me.

"Uh, no." I said. "Why do you ask?"

"Would you like to?" His hazel green eyes brightened.

"Sure. . . sounds fun!" I replied quickly, and with far too much enthusiasm. *Try not to sound quite so desperate,* I chastised myself.

"Great. . .that will be our second date!" he said confidently. "I'll set it up."

"Have we had our first yet? Date, I mean. Have we had our first date?"

"Of course, this is it!"

"A random meeting at a street dance was our first date? Not setting the bar very high, are we?"

"Nothing random about it." Luke replied. "You were meant to meet me." Confidence was never a problem for Luke.

The very next day, he picked me up in his father's 1970 pale yellow Chevy Nova. He walked up to my front door, but I quickly ran out before he had a chance to meet my parents. I wasn't ready to deal with that scenario yet. He opened the passenger side door for me, and as he walked around to the driver's side, I leaned over and unlocked his door for him.

"Thanks," he said with a huge smile. His eyes lit up in the most amazing way when he spoke, even more so when he smiled. I was mesmerized. He climbed into his seat, turned the ignition key, but the car wouldn't start. After a couple of tries, Luke opened the hood, and stuck a pen in the butterfly trap of the air filter so the car would start. The process didn't seem to faze him, nor did he seem embarrassed by it. It just was. That's how things were with him. He didn't care about his car. It was just a mode of transportation. I didn't care about his car either. I was just happy to be with him. It felt as if we had known each other for years instead of days.

We drove a half hour to the horse ranch, listening to the radio on the car stereo. *MMMBop* came on, and Luke quickly changed the station.

"Not a Hanson fan, I take it?" I asked.

"Not really. I'm more of a rock 'n roll kind of guy. You?" He replied.

"I'm a little more eclectic. Jewel, U2, The Cure, Modern English. . .stuff like that," I said.

"Interesting mix," Luke replied. "I'm going to enjoy getting to know all about you, Sarah Kent."

My loss for words was covered up by our arrival to the horse ranch. We pulled into the parking lot and were greeted by a large woman in snug denim jeans. She wore a straw cowboy hat and a red bandana around her neck over a western style button down shirt covered in a variety of stains. Occupational hazard of working a horse ranch I suppose. She walked with us to the front porch of the ranch office, and introduced herself as Tess. She asked me if I had ever ridden a horse. I shook my head, and looked at Luke, as if I needed his advice on what to say to the woman. This was his area of expertise, not mine. Luke stepped in and asked Tess for a gentle mare for me and a younger gelding for himself. Tess smiled warmly, and handed us some paperwork to fill out while she left to gather the horses. We sat at the counter and filled out the waivers. The waivers read that we agreed to not sue the ranch should we suffer injury or death while riding at their establishment. *That's encouraging*, I thought. Luke noticed my mood and asked if I was okay. I nodded my head, suddenly nervous and unable to speak, at least not without making a fool of myself. That kind of thing happened to me all the time. Give me 20 minutes to think of just the right thing to say, and I could come up with a witty comment or the perfect reply, but in the moment when I needed it. . .nothing. I opted for silence over an awkward reply.

"You sure you're okay?" he asked again, noticing my continued silence.

"Um, yeah. . .no, I'm fine. Just a little nervous, I guess. I've never been near a horse."

"Well, no worries, I have. . .lots. I used to show horses at the Equine Club. We'll make sure Tess gets you a real gentle horse. And I'll be right there with you. You are going to love it." There went his eyes again, shining with excitement. That made me more nervous than the horses. It occurred to me, what if I hated horseback riding? What if I fell right off and made a total fool of myself? Worse yet, what if this was how I died this time around? Bucked from a horse, broken neck. The headline would read: "*Young Woman with No Business on a Horse Dies Trying to Impress Boyfriend.*" Granted, it would have to be a really slow news day. Hopefully it would be a quick, painless death. The ranch would be glad I signed their waiver. I squeezed my eyes shut tightly, forcing the image of my possible demise from my head. I felt something nudge my knee and I opened my eyes. A big black dog had come over to me and was pushing his snout into my leg. I petted his head, and he pushed even closer.

"Oh, give him any lovin' and he'll never leave your side," Tess said when she noticed the dog by me. "That's Skip. He's a lover, alright."

I continued petting his thick black fur and said to Luke, "I wish I could take him home with me. He's beautiful."

Tess called out from the side of the stables, "Just leave your paperwork on the counter, and come on out here. I've got your horses all saddled up and ready to ride."

Luke opened the door for me, and I stepped out on to the side porch of the ranch house. Standing there were two beautiful brown quarter horses. Up close they were so much larger than I had imagined they would be. Mine was named Mouse. She had a white mark on her nose and big brown eyes. Luke's horse was named Voodoo. He was a lighter brown color than Mouse, and Tess had to keep a tight rein on him just to hold him while we walked to join her.

Tess looked at me and said "Mouse is a real good girl. Don't you worry sweetheart," probably assuming I needed reassurance. "Voodoo here has more spirit, but I know you can handle him, Luke." Tess apparently already knew Luke. I was first up. Luke explained how to climb up on the horse, and it was much easier to get up in the saddle than I expected. Luke smiled, pleasantly surprised, and then climbed up on to Voodoo. Normally the ranch would only allow guided trail rides, but Luke could be very convincing, and Tess knew him well enough to confidently send us on our way, with only a reminder to stick to the trails and be back before dusk.

"Just sit in the saddle and try to relax. The horse will feel it if you're tense, so try to stay loose." It was easy for him to say. "We'll take it slow. No one expects you to gallop on your first ride."

Luke gave Voodoo a gentle nudge with the heel of his boot and the horse started to walk. My horse followed Voodoo, and we rode down the trail into a wooded area in the distance. It was then I was hit by the strangest feeling. I was calm. Almost tranquil. This felt *familiar*. Mouse must have felt it too, because soon we picked up the pace, and quickly accelerated down the path. We passed Luke and Voodoo and disappeared into the woods. Luke must have assumed I was out of control, because he quickly rode up beside me with a panicked look on his face. His concern faded when he realized I was in perfect control of the horse, and more than that, I was smiling. It was a ridiculously huge smile. I felt so free. We came to a clearing in the woods. I gave Mouse a gentle squeeze with my legs, and we took off into a full gallop. I was so used to feeling trapped, even though it was by my own existence, that I'd forgotten what it felt like to be free. In that moment, on the back of that beautiful horse with the light brown eyes and a mane the color of dark chocolate, I felt liberated from my life in syndication. Suddenly I wanted to do more than just go through the motions. I wanted to live my life for real.

When the ride came to an end and we were back at the stables, Luke walked over to help me down from the saddle.

"Let me help you," he said "although I don't think you need it. I thought you said you hadn't ridden before."

"I haven't," I replied. "Beginner's luck I guess." Luke looked at me, slightly skeptical and certainly bewildered, and while reaching for my hand, caught the sleeve of his jacket on a fence nail, tearing the cuff almost an inch.

"Dang, this is my favorite jacket."

"Don't worry," I replied. "It adds character. Makes you look tough."

"Yeah," Luke laughed. "Anyone asks, I'll say it was a knife fight."

CHAPTER 5

MORE LUKE

And so it went for the next 422 days, 12 hours and 17 minutes. Luke and I were inseparable. We met for breakfast every day before our classes at the U of M, usually snuck in a quick lunch date, and then met up again at the end of the day, not parting company until the wee hours of the morning. Luke loved cooking and tried to teach me the finer points of the culinary world. It was a futile effort. I couldn't even get ice cubes from the freezer without dropping at least one. Every time, without fail. Yet he tried, and I loved the time we spent in the kitchen. I loved the time we spent anywhere. Luke loved hiking and tried to teach me how to navigate my way around the woods. I, in turn, taught him the importance of having lollipops available at all times, and the fastest, most surefire way to find poison ivy. After a good slathering of hydrocortisone cream, we drove to the place that had become our spot. Past the city lights, into the countryside, past the Afton Ski lift, and down towards the marina. We would park his car, climb on to the hood, and gaze up at the night sky looking for shooting stars. We talked about what we wanted to do with our lives, where we wanted to go, and what we wanted to see.

"I've always, always wanted to see Greece. One day I will sit on a white sand beach, look out at the bluest waters imaginable, and smell the ocean spray. Then a very handsome Greek boy will bring me a glass of pinot grigio."

"Hey! Where am I while this Greek god is bringing my girlfriend wine?" Luke asked.

"You're there. . . you just went to the store or something," I giggled as I replied. "Besides, what could Petros offer me that you don't have?"

"Oh, you're going down!" He said and pulled me off the hood of the car onto the ground. We came crashing down with a soft thud.

We were laughing and then I blurted out, "I love you Luke." I had never said it before. As I lay on the ground by the front tire of his car, in what seemed an endless pause on his part, I tried to think of what I could say to let him off the hook. It wasn't his fault if he didn't love me yet. Maybe it was too soon. Maybe he had been hurt before and was scared. Maybe I was delusional, and he didn't feel any of the same things I did. Or maybe he needed to say something. Soon.

"I think I love you, too," he finally spoke. Not a resounding declaration, but much better than the responses that had been playing through my head during the awkward silence.

One night after a late class, Luke and I planned to meet downtown for a concert. *The Cure*, one of my all-time favorite bands, was playing at First Avenue. Luke wasn't a huge fan but tolerated them for my sake. I waited for him outside the front entrance, but he was running late. I knew we would never find each other inside the crowded club once the band started, so I continued to wait outside. Soon, the line dwindled to nothing, and the doors were shut. I stood outside, sure that he would arrive any minute. I walked down the side of the building, looking at the stars painted on the outside wall, each bearing the name of a band that had performed at the famous venue. It was warm out, so I didn't mind the wait. I could hear the opening number reverberating through the walls. It was *Lovesong*. My favorite. It figured that would be the one I missed. Humming along with the song in my head, I noticed something out of the corner of my eye. It was a man. He was about 20 feet away, just standing there looking at me. More like staring at me. I started to get very uncomfortable and decided it would be better to wait for Luke inside. I made my way back to the front entrance, but he was able to close the distance between me and the doors, cutting me off and blocking my way. He reeked of whiskey and cigarette smoke. He grabbed my left arm and poked me in the back with something that felt pointy and sharp.

"Don't scream or I'll cut you right here. You're coming with me."

"Like hell I am!" I screamed. And then it happened. I started moving, swift and deliberately. It was unlike anything I had done before, yet somehow it felt completely familiar. In one seamless motion, I twisted around to the left and kicked him in the knee. He started to fall, and buckled forward as his knee gave out from beneath him. I struck his face with my right knee, and holding him up, took my right elbow and struck his jawbone, somehow knowing that was the ideal placement for the final blow. Each movement flowed from one into the next. He crumpled to the ground, writhing in agony, and called me every foul name in the book. There was blood coming out of his mouth and nose. His face was already swelling to a hideous mass of contorted flesh. He looked awful. I, on the other hand, felt amazing. Adrenaline was rushing through my entire body, with an odd mix of elation and nausea. I was still catching my breath when I heard Luke's voice. He had walked up just as I was kneeing my assailant in the face, and was close enough to see me finish with the elbow strike.

"Sarah! Are you okay? Are you hurt?" Luke asked, with a panic I had never heard in his voice.

"It's alright Luke. I'm fine. He didn't hurt me."

"Are you sure? Are you bleeding? Is that your blood?" Luke asked worriedly.

"Oh, yeah, I guess it is. He must have nicked my arm a little with his knife. I guess it does sting now a bit after all," I replied.

Before Luke could say anything more, the police and ambulance arrived. Upon Luke's insistence, one of the paramedics from the ambulance looked at my arm. It could have used some stitches, but the paramedic said if I didn't mind having a scar, he could seal it up right there with some medical glue and tape. I agreed, not wanting to waste anymore of this night at the hospital instead of being with Luke.

Luke was staring at me. "Where did you learn to fight like that? When did you learn to do that?" In this case, "*When*" was the more appropriate question.

"Um, my dad," I lied and tried to think of a more believable response than *in a past life*. "He taught me some self-defense in high school. I guess it just came back to me."

"I'll say it did. I could kick myself. You were waiting for me. . . this is my fault. I don't know what I would have done if something had happened to you."

"It's okay. I'm fine Luke, really, I am."

"I just want to take you home, where I know you're safe. Besides, there's something I need to ask you," he said rather cryptically.

"Can't you ask me now? What's up? Is something wrong?" I asked, completely forgetting my injuries.

"No," Luke replied. "Nothing's wrong. This is something I need to ask you in the right way. Let's take care of the rest of this unpleasantness now, I'll drive you home, and then we'll start fresh tomorrow. Meet me for breakfast? Say, 8:30 at our usual place?"

"It's a date. 8:30 at Al's," I replied.

I finished giving my statement to the police and Luke drove me back to my house. My parents weren't home, and it was just as well. I didn't want to fumble through an explanation of how I was able to fend off my attacker, although I knew I would have to tell them eventually. Tonight, I just wanted to crawl into bed and dream of Luke. He had said he had something important to ask me. He wanted to ask me something, and said it had to be done the right way. It didn't take much for my heart to convince my head that Luke was going to propose to me in the morning. We would have a great story for our kids someday about how their father asked their mother to marry him at Al's Breakfast. We would leave out the part about the knife fight at First Avenue the night before. Instead we would tell them about Al's, the tiny diner, with all of 14 seats. It had become a quick favorite for us from the very first time we went there, starving after a long all-nighter of studying. I loved the buttermilk waffles and would eat them daily if given the opportunity. I would dip them in my orange juice, which paired perfectly with the maple syrup.

"What are you doing to that poor waffle?" Luke would ask.

"What? Lots of people dip their waffles," I replied.

"Lots of people dip their waffles in syrup. What you're doing is just wrong," Luke said, with a slightly disgusted look on his face.

"Hey, don't knock it until you've tried it," I dared him.

Luke gave in and tried O.J. dipped waffles, and said "Yeah, that's horrible."

"It's not my fault your palate isn't as refined as mine," I laughed.

Not even thoughts of Al's amazing waffles could distract me from wondering about what Luke was going to ask me tomorrow. I went to bed and when I finally fell asleep, I dreamt of Luke.

CHAPTER 6

BREAKFAST AT AL'S DINER

The next morning, I didn't need an alarm to wake me. I had been waiting for the sun to rise so I could start what I was sure would be the best day of my life, possibly of all my lives. I spent far too much time deciding what to wear, finally choosing a yellow sundress, mostly because Luke had commented one time how much he liked it. I wore my hair down and put on the necklace he had given me when we first started dating. It was only a couple of months after we'd been horseback riding. We went to the Minnesota Zoo to see the dolphin show. After watching Semo the dolphin perform some truly amazing tricks, and flipping several feet out of the water, Luke stopped in the gift shop and bought me a silver necklace with a small dolphin pendant.

He put it around my neck and said, "The way Semo jumped out of the water is what you do to my heart every time I see you." It was sappy, but I loved every word. I loved him. I couldn't help but wonder what he would say this morning, how he would propose.

The telephone ringing snapped me out of my daydream. It was my mom asking me to stop by the bank to deposit her paycheck. I told her I was going to meet Luke for breakfast, but I could do it on my way. She said it was by the breadbox in the kitchen and thanked me profusely for saving her from another shiny moment. That was what my mom called it when she got distracted and forgot to do something. I told her it was no problem, and I would see her tonight at dinner.

"Ok, thanks again sweetheart. Love you."

"Love you too, Mom." I hurried out the door, and grabbed my purse and sweater on the way out. It wasn't exactly sundress weather, but with the light sweater I would be warm enough. *Besides*, I thought to myself, *if Luke was going to ask me what I thought he was, I doubt I would have even noticed a blizzard.*

I pulled up to the curb by Al's Diner, put change in the meter, and quickly crossed the street to the bank. I looked back and could see Luke inside the diner already. He was sitting at the table by the window. He hadn't seen me yet, so I just stood there looking at him for a minute. I wanted to soak in everything about this moment. I could smell the freshly baked rolls coming from inside the diner, and the coffee from the stand next door. The sky was clear and blue, without a single cloud in sight. Luke looked out the window and caught my eye. I smiled and he smiled back. I motioned to the bank, pointing to the door of the building and then over to Luke. He nodded his head, letting me know that he understood my crude form of sign language, that I would be joining him shortly. I opened the bank door and looked back one more time across the street to Luke. I flashed what I hoped was an unforgettable smile, then turned to go inside.

The bank was busy that morning, filled with people trying to take care of their errands before work. I looked for the shortest line, anxious to get to the diner, to Luke and his question for me. I was so lost in my anticipation I didn't notice the man with the heavy trench coat walking quickly up to a teller. I was still daydreaming about Luke, and what I had thought might be a small black box on the table in front of him, when heavy trench coat guy pulled out a shotgun.

He screamed "EVERYONE ON THE GROUND. . . NOW! NO ONE MOVES, AND NO ONE HAS TO DIE." He pointed the gun right at the teller. She started to cry hysterically. "GET ALL THE MONEY OUT OF THE DRAWER NOW, OR YOU DIE!"

The teller shook frantically but opened her cash drawer and began taking out the money. I was on the floor, trying not to move a muscle. From the corner of my eye I could see a mother with her little boy, trying to comfort him and keep him still. Our eyes met, and I could see the fear in her eyes was clearly not for her own safety. She was terrified for the life of her little boy. He started to cry, and his sobs caught the attention of the armed robber.

"SHUT HIM UP NOW!" He shouted. His bellowing only frightened the boy more, and he started to wail. I reached into my purse to grab a lollipop. My fingers fumbled around my hairbrush, wallet, something with string, and then landed on a lollipop. I stretched my arm out to the mother of the little boy, extending the lollipop to her to give to her son. It was same moment the bank guard chose to make his move against the robber. The robber heard the guard draw his firearm, and in a flash of gunfire and chaos, the robber fired his weapon. The guard took a hit to the knee, firing his gun at the same time, hitting the robber in the chest. He dropped to the floor, and as he fell, he fired one last shot. It wasn't until I saw the look on the young mother's face, then saw her shield her son's eyes that I knew. The blood from the hole through my chest seeped out quickly, soaking my yellow sundress. I didn't feel anything at first, then all I felt was cold. My life as Sarah Kent ended at 20 years old, on a cold bank floor, hoping to comfort a little boy. Being with Luke was the only time I can remember not caring about what happened in my other lives, and it had ended too soon.

CHAPTER 7

DULUTH/SARAH DALEY

In this life, my current life as Sarah Daley, the *moment* hit me four years ago, when I just turned 15. I don't know why I am always named Sarah. It's yet another thing out of my control. Maybe it was just a coincidence, or maybe it meant something. It certainly wasn't one of my biggest problems.

I lived in Duluth, Minnesota, which was a beautiful town filled with amazing scenery, located on the shores of the vast Lake Superior. There were amazing hiking trails, quaint coffee shops, bakeries, and even a ship with full sails in the harbor. I loved running down by the water's edge. It was during a long run when the *moment* hit me. It was late October, and I knew it would probably be my last shot at a decent run outside before the true cold of winter set in. Once it did, it wouldn't release its icy grip for the next five months, maybe more, so I wanted this last run in a bad way.

I found my favorite socks, put on my warm running pants, borrowed my dad's long sleeve Vikings T-shirt and quickly got dressed. I grabbed my iPod, wristwatch, and ID wristband my dad gave me. He insisted I wear one when I run, in case I got hit by a car or something, I guess. I started out on the street in front of our house on Grand Avenue and headed toward the harbor. *Tear in My Heart* by Twenty-one Pilots played on my iPod, and I quickly found my stride. It was the pace that helped me clear my head, sort out problems or just not think about anything. The wind whipped up, making the 50-degree afternoon feel more like 40. I pulled the sleeves of my dad's shirt down over my hands to keep my fingers warm. The music changed to *I Melt With You.* Modern English was a throwback to a previous life, and it was still my favorite song. One mile into my run, the rain started. I thought about turning back, but it was only sprinkling, and I really wanted this run, so I kept on going. The raindrops started to fall faster, and grew colder, pelting me in the face as I ran. I had to keep blinking my eyes just to see where I was going.

A big garbage truck drove past, and made the leaves on the street swirl up and fly around me. I loved the wild feel of the wind when I was running. Soon, an even larger truck drove by, and again the leaves flew up in the air, but it was different this time. It was odd. The leaves swirled up, but they took much longer to settle back to the ground. They seemed to float, suspended in the air. Then a car went by, but as if it was in slow motion. I blinked my eyes hard, and tried to clear my vision. I thought the mist was playing tricks on me. The leaves kept swirling around me in slow motion, suspended in the air. It was as if everything around me was blurred, and blending in with the surroundings. I couldn't tell one tree from the next, or the sky from the ground. Then I hit the ground.

When I woke, I was lying in a hospital bed, and surrounded by nurses. Everything was still blurry. I blinked hard again to try and focus. A nurse with dark brown hair saw me open my eyes and said, "She's awake." Another nurse, an older woman with blonde hair walked over to me, leaned over my bedside, and moved my hair across my forehead and out of my eyes. She had pale blue eyes and smelled like peppermint.

"Hi honey. You've got a fairly large goose egg on your head. How are you feeling? Can you tell me your name?" she asked me.

Huh. My name. Simple enough request. I should be able to do that, I thought. My head was aching and fuzzy, so it took me a couple of seconds to answer.

"Um, it's Sarah."

"Okay, that's good. That's really good. Sarah what?" the blonde nurse asked.

Huh. Another fuzzy wave went through my head.

"Um, Kent. Sarah Kent."

The nurse with the brown hair looked at my wrist and noticed the ID wristband my dad had given me.

"This says her name is Sarah Daley."

The blonde nurse who smelled like peppermint asked me again.

"Honey, could you tell me your name one more time?"

"Yes, it's Sarah Kent. I think, I. . .I mean, I'm not sure."

"Her parents will be here soon. Seeing them should help her," the dark-haired nurse said.

"Don't worry honey, you are going to be fine," she said. I wasn't so sure.

By the time my parents arrived, I knew who I was. I knew I was Sarah Daley, and I was a sophomore at Duluth High School. I knew I lived on Grand Avenue. I knew my parents were Bob and Karen Daley. I knew the last song I heard on my iPod was *I Melt With You*. I didn't know why I'd said my name was Sarah Kent. After a CT scan to rule out brain trauma, the doctors released me to my parents with instructions to watch me closely for signs of concussion. My dad spent the entire ride home reiterating how important the ID wristband had been, and how glad he was that he'd bought it for me.

"Now you understand why I wanted you to wear it. I can't believe you went so long without one. Thank goodness you were wearing it today. When I think of what could have happened. . ." It was a long car ride home. I tuned him out around the third "thank goodness." I stared out the window into the dark night; the silhouette of the trees against the midnight blue sky blurred together. It was the same way the trees had blurred during my run. *Sarah Kent,* I thought. I didn't know why I said my name was Sarah Kent. The lump on my head began to throb and I groaned softly as I touched it. It was still loud enough for my mom to hear, even over my father's ongoing testimonial to the virtues of proper identification.

"How's your head, baby? Is it still really hurting?" she asked.

"Oh, it's not so bad," I lied to her. In truth, it was pounding.

"Well, the doctor said it would for a few days. We'll have to wake you a few times tonight to make sure you're okay. How did you fall anyway?" she asked.

"I just twisted my ankle and lost my balance," I lied again. Not my most graceful *moment.*

While Duluth is beautiful, it is also certainly one of the coldest places I'd ever lived. Today was another morning of snow. I'm not sure how long it had been since I thought the snow was beautiful, or appreciated how lovely it was, falling gently from the sky and dusting the trees. Now it was just cold. I kept living all these lives but felt less alive with each one.

Yet, there were some advantages to living multiple lives. It didn't take long after the *moment* hit, and I remembered almost everything about the last life, including everything I learned in high school, college, and sometimes beyond. This time around, I was 15 when the moment struck. I got past the initial confusion, shock, and headache, and found I was academically gifted for my age. My teachers were amazed at how quickly I accelerated. They tested me for advanced placement, and I ended up skipping a few grades. I didn't mind. I was anxious to get past the parts of life I had already lived so many times before. I didn't have many friends. Making friends was hard to do when everyone thought I was either a little off, or too shy. Skipping ahead was no worse than staying with my classmates. That's why I'm 19 and a senior in college in my final year at the University of Minnesota-Duluth.

Today was another morning of snow. I woke to my roommate Chloe complaining *again*. Chloe was a nice girl but complained constantly. This time it was about our apartment décor.

"This carpet is beyond ugly, and why would anyone paint walls this color? It's absolutely hideous," she grumbled.

In her defense, the wall color was awful, and accentuated even more by the small space that made up our living quarters.

"Oh, it's not so bad. Hey, at least it's not white," I replied.

I put on my ridiculously huge North Face parka, my Sorel snow boots, and grabbed my backpack to head out toward the English building. It was on the other side of campus from my apartment, but I was a teacher assistant in the English Department for Professor Briggs, so I couldn't be late. Professor Briggs' wife was very pregnant with their first child. They had been trying for a baby for almost eight years, so naturally he was very excited, often chattering on for hours about every baby topic imaginable.

"You have to be sure to provide the right type of stimulation. You want the proper amount as well. Too little and the baby could lose interest, too much and the baby will become over stimulated. And you wouldn't believe all the theories on 'crying it out'. . . don't even get me started."

No worries, I won't, I thought. I tried to feign interest for his sake. He was a wonderful teacher, and a truly kind man. I wished I could feel more excitement for him, but in all honesty, I had to force myself to pay attention. I didn't know if it was because I'd never had a child—not that I could recall anyway—or perhaps because I might never live long enough to have one, but I couldn't identify with that kind of joy. At least not anymore.

When I tuned back in, Professor Briggs was still talking about baby stuff, apparently not noticing that I hadn't been paying attention.

"I just hope I don't cry like a big baby when she's born," he said to me.

"I'm sure no one would mind, and I doubt you would be the first," I replied, trying to say the right thing. Truth was, I envied him. I couldn't remember the last time I cried. I'd been in plenty of situations where it would have been appropriate, even expected for me to cry. Funerals, weddings, saying goodbye to friends moving away to school, but I had yet to shed even one tear in this lifetime. I would go through the motions, but never really felt it. It was like I was acting out a role, starring in the motion picture of my life, but with no cameras rolling, no world premiere, and no red carpet.

I got to the lecture room just as the last class was leaving. *Perfect timing,* I thought. I wouldn't have to answer any questions. A fellow T.A. asked me to grade his stack of essays so he could take off a day early. . . I didn't mind. There was nothing urgent waiting for me. There wasn't anything waiting for me.

CHAPTER 8

STUCK IN THE PAST

Probably the hardest part of living one life after another, other than living through high school over and over again, was waiting. No, I take that back. The hardest thing was knowing I'd have to wait. When the *moment* hit, all the glimpses of the past turned to clear, vivid memories. In all my lives, I'd only fallen in love once, with Luke. So here I was, living yet another life and feeling rather stuck. I got better at sorting out the memories; at first, they were like several puzzles mixed up together in one big box. Over time, I could fit them in with my current life. Only this time, I couldn't get past one piece of the puzzle. I couldn't get past Luke. I could still see his face, his pale, hazel green eyes searing with intensity. I could still feel his soft lips, and the way kissed me. I closed my eyes, took a deep breath, and smelled his cologne. The same scent that comforted me so many nights when I wore one of his shirts to sleep in when we were apart.

I kept looking for him, thinking somehow this time, in this life, I'd find him again. I couldn't be the only one repeating my existence. *I must get over him, or I'm not sure how I will ever continue living one life after another.* Not that I had a choice. For all I knew, I could be immortal. If I was, it was kind of a crappy way of doing it. It was more like being stuck in a game with never-ending do-overs. I had so many questions about my existence, but where I went from here was one question I couldn't seem to answer.

Sometimes I'd see his face. I'd spot him in a crowd or through a store window. I used to run into the store, only to be disappointed, and realizing the image was only in my mind. Now, I just stared at the window, willing his image to stay, holding on to any reminder of him I can. It felt useless. I'd spent my entire existence always looking to the next life, missing out on what was going on around me. I never fully appreciated living in the present until I met Luke. Now without him in my new life, I wasn't sure how to live at all. It was like never being able to get a full breath. My life became an echo. . . a pale, fading copy of the original.

AMY LARSON MARBLE

CHAPTER 9

DO-OVER

Being emotionally unavailable made life easier, with no fear of getting close to someone, only to lose them. It was easier to keep people at a distance. I didn't care if the other college students thought I was unapproachable, cold, or aloof. I overheard one girl call me "dead inside." Her assessment wasn't that far off.

My professor told me it was my lack of friends that made me the ideal choice to be his teaching assistant. He wasn't intending to be unkind, he just meant there was no concern of my going easy on friends in the class while grading papers. As we got to know each other through the months, Professor Briggs and I got to be friends, of sorts. He was more like a favorite uncle than my professor, and he often expressed concern over my lack of social interaction.

"It's not like I'm suggesting you hit a kegger, Sarah. I just think it would do you good to join people your own age, doing things people your age do."

"Things people my age do? You realize most people my age are complete idiots, right? Why do you think I hang out in your classroom all the time?"

"And I am lucky to have your company, but soon I'll be on family leave and you'll be here on your own," he replied.

"I do fine on my own, but thanks Professor. Besides, I'll still be the T.A. for this class, won't I?"

"Absolutely. I wouldn't replace you, but my replacement isn't known for his outgoing personality. He's a very quiet man. I don't know if you'll have anyone to talk with if you keep spending all your time in this classroom."

Suits me fine, I thought. "When will he be taking over for you?" I asked.

"Well, today actually. Debra is nervous about going into early labor, so I've moved up my leave to start tomorrow. Professor Taylor will be here in about 15 minutes if you would like me to handle the introductions?"

"Sure, why not?" I replied with a complete lack of enthusiasm.

"Alright then, I'll run tomorrow's quiz down to the copier while you finish grading today's assignment, and he should be here by the time I return." He was still talking as he walked out of the classroom, barely missing the door frame with his head as he turned down the hallway.

Hopefully the baby will have Debra's coordination, I said to myself.

The next 15 minutes dragged on as I read yet another essay on *Beowulf*, this one comparing the epic saga to the Arnold Schwarzenegger movie version of *Conan the Barbarian*. I had too much on my mind to try to wrap my head around the parallels between the classic tale of mortal man's triumph over evil and a pre-terminator Arnie. All I could think was "I'll be back. . ." in a thick Austrian accent.

"I'm back." Professor Briggs had returned. "Has Professor Taylor stopped in yet?"

"Uh, no, not yet. I can always meet him tomorrow. I should get going anyway, and you should be getting home to Debra," I told him. And then he walked in. Professor Taylor. Professor Luke Taylor. Luke. My Luke.

I stood behind Professor Briggs' desk, mouth gaping, and unable to speak. Not quite the description Professor Taylor had received about the intelligent, well-spoken teaching assistant who would be helping him with the mid-semester transition.

"Luke," I whispered more than spoke.

"I'm sorry. . . have you two already met?" Professor Briggs asked, a bit surprised by my recognition of the man in the doorway.

"Uh, no, I mean, no. I, uh, just. . . no," I stammered.

There was no chance of being well spoken now. The best I could manage was barely coherent. I couldn't believe it. I was staring at the man I had loved more than I ever thought possible. The man I wanted to marry and have kids with, and swing on a porch chair with when we were old. The man who was now almost 20 years older than me. *Whoa.* He still looked the same. How could he still look the same? Except for a few more wrinkles, a little less hair with a sprinkling of grey, he was the same. Yet there was something very different about him now.

There was a sadness in his eyes. He wasn't the same Luke who had smiled at me from the diner, before I went into the bank that day, almost two decades ago.

Apparently, I had been staring long enough to make everyone uncomfortable, so Professor Briggs graciously spoke up.

"Okay, introductions. Sarah Daley, Professor Luke Taylor. Professor Taylor, this is my wonderful teaching assistant, whom without I simply could not manage. Now that the introductions are done, I must run. Sarah, would you please be kind enough to help Professor Taylor settle in?"

"Uh, sure, I'd be glad to!" I replied with far too much enthusiasm.

Luke, apparently creeped out by my freakish staring, said it wasn't necessary, but Professor Briggs insisted, assuring him he was in good hands with his favorite T.A.

"She's brilliant, although she'll never admit to it. I know you two will get along splendidly. So, I'm off then. Good luck to you both, and wish me luck. . .I'm going to be a father!" With that, Professor Briggs was out the door and I was left alone with Luke. I was with Luke. I still couldn't believe it.

"Perhaps you could help me carry some of my books in from my car?' Luke asked.

"Uh, sure. I'd, uh, be glad to," I practically stuttered.

Think of something to say, Sarah, I chastised myself. *He's going to think you're a complete idiot.* As we made our way out to the staff parking lot, I decided I wouldn't speak again, at least not until I got a grip, although I had no idea of how to do that. I couldn't wrap my head around this situation. This is the man, who the last time I saw him, was going to ask me to marry him, and I was going to say yes. Granted, that was 20 years ago, but still, it was a big deal. Now we were together again, only he had no clue who I was. Right then, I wasn't sure either.

I started to ask him where he was from, deciding small talk was my best bet at the time. It didn't seem right to start out with "By the way, you probably don't remember me, since I look different and have a different name, and oh yeah, it was 20 years ago, and technically I wasn't born yet, but you love me and want to marry me." That probably wouldn't have been the best opener. Then it occurred to me; he was probably already married. It would only make sense. He was amazing. Kind, intelligent, funny, handsome. . . he was probably married with a family. I had to find out. I had found my opener.

"So, are you from Duluth?" I asked, totally chickening out.

"No, not originally. I grew up in Minneapolis. I moved around after college, and just settled here last year. How about you?" he asked. The tone in his voice rang of courtesy more than actual interest.

"It's complicated," I replied, kicking myself almost immediately for my lame response.

"Where you're from is complicated? Professor Briggs said you were interesting. Oh, that's my car on the end, the black Nova."

"You drive a Chevy Nova?" I asked.

"Yeah, my first car was a Nova. I've had others, but I always come back to the Chevys. You never forget your first car. Just like your first love, I guess. Um, sorry. I don't know why I said that. Anyway, in answer to your question, yes, I drive a Chevy Nova." He seemed embarrassed and a bit flustered. A slight smile crept across my face.

He hadn't forgotten me.

CHAPTER 10

GETTING TO KNOW LUKE AGAIN

And so, it began, my second meeting with my first love was off to a bumpy, but promising start. As we loaded our arms with books from his car, I asked him if his wife was from Minneapolis as well.

"I'm not married actually," he replied.

"Oh?" I replied.

"No, is that so odd?"

"No, not odd, just surprising I guess," I struggled for a witty reply, falling painfully short. So much for my promising start.

"I was close once. I even had the ring. But sometimes life doesn't turn out like you expect." He looked distant and sad as he replied. "Enough of that, though," he said before I could stick my foot any further in my mouth. "Let's get these books back to the lecture hall so you can get on with your weekend. I'm sure you have better things to do than hang around the classroom on a Friday night." He couldn't have been more wrong. Hit with a desperate need to be near him, I struggled to find an excuse to stay.

"Actually, my plans fell through, so I'd be glad to help you some more, that is, if you need it," I said, holding my breath for his reply.

"Well, I suppose, if you've nothing else to do, I could use the help."

It wasn't *"Yes, stay, stay forever,"* but it was a beginning. It took two more trips to the Nova to haul the textbooks to the classroom.

"Why are you changing textbooks mid-semester?" I asked, out of genuine curiosity rather than desperation to talk to him. It was a nice change of pace.

"I'm not changing the textbook; I'm just adding this one to the curriculum," he replied.

"Oh, you're going to be famously popular. . . nothing like an additional textbook to make the student body love you. I know I could always use more homework." My sarcastic tone was not lost on him.

"Well, it's not required for testing. I wrote it. I just thought it would bring another point of view to the classroom discussion," he replied, a little taken back by my remark.

"You wrote this?" I held the heavy book in my hands. I hadn't even looked at it yet. The cover was a picture of the bluest ocean with a white sand beach. Just beyond the beach were white houses with bright blue rooftops. They looked as if they had sprung from the hillside, more a part of the landscape than structures on top of it. It was Greece. I smiled again. He really hadn't forgotten me.

We carried the rest of his supplies to his office, and once the pencil cup and in-box tray had been placed on his desk with a few helpful suggestions where they would look better and be more accessible, I decided to take a leap.

"I don't know about you, but I could really use some coffee. Want to go grab a cup? We could talk about your curriculum?" I asked, with more enthusiasm than a curriculum conversation would warrant.

"I appreciate all the help you've given me, Sarah, but I really should call it a night. I have a big day tomorrow and should try to get some decent sleep," he replied.

"Oh, big day?" I asked, not willing to let go just yet. "What are you doing? If you don't mind me asking?"

"I am getting a dog. I've been meaning to do it for a while now, so this time tomorrow I will be the proud owner of a black Labrador retriever. I'm adopting him from a rescue shelter, and I have to leave by 6:00 a.m. to pick him up."

"Want some company?" I blurted out, hoping it didn't sound as desperate out loud as it did in my head.

"Uh, sure, I guess," he replied. I had caught him off guard with my offer to accompany him.

"Okay, great! I'll meet you at your place at 5:30." I said quickly, not wanting to give him time to change his mind or come up with an excuse to back out.

"Okay. See you then I guess." He replied, looking a bit bewildered.

"Okay, goodnight then. Nice meeting you." I could barely contain the smile bursting across my face. *Nice to meet you again, Luke.*

I went home to my apartment, feeling more content than I had in years. Seeing Luke again opened a part of me that I had locked away long ago. I had hope again for something more than an endless existence of isolation. I didn't know how I would tell him about me, about us, and our life together that had been cut short. Then it hit me. . . I wasn't sure if I should tell him. Perhaps it was selfish of me to want to start another life with him. After all, I was already 19 years old with possibly only four more years left in this life, not to mention he was 20 years older than me. Although technically, I was hundreds of years older than him. He might not believe me, no matter what I tell him, and after a well-intentioned phone call placed to my parents, I would end up in a room with white padded walls again. It was too much to think about now, and I wanted to enjoy this happy moment a bit longer. I put it out of my head and focused on seeing him again tomorrow. I went to bed that night and dreamt of Luke. It was the best night's sleep I had had in a very long time.

CHAPTER 11

ROAD TRIP

I showed up at Luke's door the next morning at 5:30 sharp, which was likely the first instance of me on time for anything, ever. I don't remember a life where I was especially punctual. It's not that I didn't care, I was just very bad at time management. But not that morning; I was there, donuts in hand, ready to rekindle my love affair with Luke. I knocked on the door, heard him yell "Come in," and stepped inside, thinking how this could be our home one day. Luke walked out from the kitchen, towel in hand.

"Just finishing up the dishes," he said.

"You do dishes at 5:30 in the morning," I said. "I didn't picture you as a neat freak."

"I'm not a neat freak, per se, I just hate clutter," he replied.

I hadn't remembered that about him from our life together when I was Sarah Kent. I had become a minimalist over the course of my lives as well. There was no point in getting attached to things I couldn't take with me to the next life. It made me wonder what else I had forgotten about Luke. I took a long look at him. He was wearing jeans, a blue T-shirt, and an old jean jacket that looked like he'd had it forever. Looking closer, I realized it was his jacket from high school. I recognized the rip on the cuff of his sleeve. It had caught on a nail at the stables when we had gone riding for our second date. Luke noticed my staring at him and asked if I was okay.

"Yeah, fine, why?" I replied.

"You were zoning out there for a minute. You looked a million miles away," he said.

No, not a million miles, I thought. *Just 20 years.*

"I need to grab my keys from the other room, be back in a second," he said.

I looked around his place while he went to the other room. A stack of boxes next to the door caught my eye. "Donate" was written in black sharpie across the side of one box, and "Sell" across another. I wasn't trying to be nosey, but soon found myself looking through the items in the box marked "Sell." There were some video games, an old and clearly worn out iPad, and a small black velvet box. It was the velvet box that caught my eye. I quickly looked over my shoulder to see if Luke had returned, and even though I knew I shouldn't, I picked up the small black box, and opened it. Inside was a beautiful ring. It had a single diamond, with a setting of white gold in the shape of two dolphins encircling the stone. Tears started to roll down my face. It had to be the ring Luke had bought to propose to me all those years ago. He had kept it all this time. At least until now, considering it was currently in a box marked "Sell." I was still holding the box in my hand when Luke returned from the other room.

"I'm sorry," I stammered, "I didn't mean to snoop. It just caught my eye." I wiped the tears away before he could notice. "You're selling it? Why?" I asked.

"Sometimes you have to move on," he said, clearly angry for my intrusion into his privacy. "We should get going if we don't want to be late," Luke said, still irritated, "we can get some coffee on the way."

I chose not to pry further. I knew all about that day anyway. I understood why he would want to move on. I had tried for years and hadn't been able.

"I'm ready to go, but I'll pass on the coffee," I replied. "Never liked the stuff. The smell is great, but it always tastes so bitter to me. I've tried everything, adding hot chocolate, even ice cream, but. . ." I realized he hadn't asked for my thoughts on caffeinated morning beverages, and I was babbling on like someone who had already had far too much coffee that morning.

"I'm good. Thanks though," I said, attempting to reel in my inner dialogue. Luke looked amused. I was grateful for the mood change.

"Don't stop talking on my account. It's amazing what you learn about people just by listening," he said.

"I'm afraid we'll need more than a two-hour car ride to cover the saga of my existence," I replied.

"No worries," he said, smiling. "We have the ride back too."

CHAPTER 12

I MELT WITH YOU

The only constant that remained from one life to the next was music. Fortunately, with the advent of streaming, my favorite songs would always be there, no matter how many lives I lived. Luke and I never shared similar taste in music, so I was surprised to hear the mix of songs on his playlist. We weren't even out of the driveway before *I Melt With You* was playing on his car stereo.

"I love this song," I said. I reached for the volume dial, looking at Luke with an expression that asked if I could turn it up.

"Yeah, go ahead," he said. "You like Modern English? A bit before your time, aren't they?"

"Modern English are timeless, and yes, they are one of my favorites," I replied.

Luke was quiet for a moment, looking as if he wanted to say something, but then thought better of it. I sat back, listening to the music, soaking in every bit of the moment I could. I tried not to be too conspicuous as I gazed at Luke from the corner of my eye. Sitting next to him in his car, comfortable in his company without needing to talk, even the smell of his aftershave, was all so familiar. It was the strongest feeling of déjà vu I had experienced in all my lives. Something told me he felt it too. Maybe it was the way I would tilt my head when I disagreed with him, or how I would sit pretzel fashion in my seat. Mannerisms from my former lives remained a part of me, and no one had known me better than Luke. The longer we drove, the stronger the feeling grew. I could sense him wanting to say something, so I broke the tension by asking him about his job.

"What made you want to become a teacher?" I asked. The Luke I knew years ago wanted to work on Wall Street.

"It wasn't what I planned to do when I started college. I was a business major originally, and wanted a career in finance," he replied.

"What changed your mind?" I asked, truly interested in learning more about what happened to him after I died.

He hesitated before answering. "I guess I needed something more meaningful." As he continued to speak, his voice trailed off and I could see the beginning of tears glistening in his eyes. "I lost someone back in college. Someone who was important to me. I guess it changed me. For the longest time, nothing seemed to matter anymore. All I felt was pain and loss, and soon I didn't want to feel anything at all. I started drinking. A lot. My family and friends were out of their minds worried about me. After a year of drifting a sea of pain, my mom was the one who brought me back. Everyone else told me to give it time, that I would find love again. My mom was the only one who said it didn't matter. She told me I had been lucky enough to be loved by someone with their whole heart and soul, and whether I ever fell in love again, I experienced the real deal. That was more than most people ever got." His voice trailed off to a near whisper. "I needed to do something with my life that would make her proud. That's when I decided to become a teacher." He realized how much he had shared with me and cleared his throat. "That's more than you asked, I'm sorry. I don't know why I told you all of that."

"No worries, I asked. So, you became a teacher just like your mom. That's really cool," I replied; a bit overcome myself by the depth of his answer.

"Did I tell you my mom was a teacher?" he asked.

"Uh, yeah, you must have. Or maybe Professor Briggs mentioned it before he left on family leave."

I remembered Luke's mom Carol. She was a high school math teacher in Saint Paul, Minnesota when Luke and I met. We hit it off immediately. We both loved Tom Hanks movies, popcorn with extra butter, and Broadway show tunes. More importantly, she could see how deeply I loved her son. She would joke saying "If that boy is ever fool enough to lose you sweetie, I will kick him to the curb myself." It didn't surprise me that she was his rock when I died. Luke and I sat quietly for the remainder of the drive, neither of us sure what to say.

CHAPTER 13

SKIP

The paved road changed to dirt, and soon we were at the farm-turned-animal-rescue shelter. Dogs of all sizes ran around. Some played while others chased a reckless squirrel who dared to trespass. Luke looked at me and gestured toward the main house, a large white farmhouse with a wraparound porch. On the front side there was a swinging chair, almost exactly like the one Sarah Mackenzie's dad had given to her mom. I had so many memories from so many lifetimes. It was no wonder things would occasionally slip, like the comment about Luke's mom being a teacher. It was too much to keep straight what I should—or shouldn't—know.

Several minutes passed with more dogs, but no people anywhere to be seen. Luke took out his cellphone to call the shelter contact, when a loud whistle followed by a deep bark came from behind the barn. A man dressed in jeans, flannel shirt, and cowboy boots, walked towards us with a beautiful black lab trailing slightly behind him. A younger man, probably in his late teens, walked beside the dog. Luke waved to the man in boots and called out to him.

"Ted! Good to see you! Is that Skip?"

"Luke, good to see you too! Yeah, that's him alright. Come on over and meet him."

"You're naming him Skip?" I asked.

"Yeah," he replied. "I think it fits him."

As we walked toward Ted, Skip, and the young man, Luke's face was transformed by a huge smile. Twenty years later, his eyes still sparkled like they did the night we met. I walked with him to meet the dog, this wonderful canine who had given me an opportunity to spend time with Luke. I loved him already.

"Ted, this is Sarah. She graciously offered to help me pick up Skip today."

"Nice to meet you Sarah," Ted replied. "Allow me to introduce you both to Vasily. He is a foreign exchange student staying with our family and has been a huge help to us at the shelter."

"Hello Vasily, it's lovely to meet you," I said.

"Hello, it is lovely to meeting you too," Vasily replied, in slightly broken but easily understood English.

"Luke, why don't we step inside and take care of the paperwork, and then you and Skip can be on your way?" Ted gestured toward the main house.

"Coming?" Luke asked me.

"I think I'll stay here with Skip and Vasily, if that's okay with both of you," I said as I pet the thick black fur on Skip's head.

"Sure, we shouldn't be too long," Luke responded as he and Ted turned and went inside. Vasily handed me a tennis ball to throw for Skip.

"You throwing for dog, yeah?" Vasily mimicked a throwing motion, in case I needed a visual aide.

"Yes please," I replied, taking the ball from Vasily and pitching it as far as I could. Skip took off, surprisingly fast for such a large dog. The ball must have landed on a slope, rolling down a small hill. Skip disappeared from view trying to retrieve it.

"*Вернись! Вернись!*" Vasily hollered after the dog to come back.

Skip came bounding back over the ridge and ran straight to Vasily and me with the tennis ball in his mouth.

"*Какая хорошая собака,*" I said, "what a good dog" to Skip, praising him for retrieving the ball.

"You speak Russian?" Vasily asked, his eyes wide with surprise and delight.

"*Да, наверное,*" I replied that I guess I did. Vasily, excited for the opportunity to speak in his native tongue, began talking quickly, waving his hands as he told me about his home back in Yaroslavl, two hours northeast of Moscow. I asked him about his family, and if it was hard being so far from home.

"*Ты скучаешь по своей семье?*" I asked Vasily if he missed his family.

"*Да, очень, но семья Теда была очень добр ко мне,*" he replied, telling me that he did, but how kind Ted and his family had been to him since he arrived.

"Ted does seem like a very nice man. I'm glad his family is taking such good care of you." We were still talking when Luke and Ted returned.

"Luke, you didn't tell me Sarah spoke Russian. I could have used her help when Vasily first arrived," Ted said, smiling at me and patting Vasily on the shoulder.

"Vasily was just telling me how wonderful you and your family have been to him since his arrival in the United States."

"We're lucky to have him here with us," Ted replied. "He's a great kid. Wonderful with the animals too."

"They say dogs are great judges of character," I replied, smiling at Vasily.

"They are indeed, Sarah. I see Skip has taken to you quite nicely." Ted pointed down to the dog who had curled up at my feet.

"We should get going," Luke chimed in. "It'll take all day to get back if we get stuck in weekend lake traffic."

We loaded Skip's dog bed and a few tennis balls in the trunk of the Nova, and opened the car door for Skip to jump in. He leapt without hesitation. I knew the feeling.

CHAPTER 14

POSSIBILITIES

L uke and I sat in the car quietly for the first few minutes, taking turns looking back at Skip to make sure the dog was okay. Then, a few miles further down the road, Luke said "Russian? You're what, 21 or 22 years old, and you speak fluent Russian?"

"I'm 19 actually," I replied. "Is a second language that unusual?"

"No, I guess not. Spanish, German, even Norwegian, but Russian is rare in these parts," Luke replied, the look on his face was a combination of disbelief and amusement.

"I'm going to enjoy getting to know you, Sarah Daley," he said. The déjà vu was palatable.

Luke had no sooner said the words, nearly identical to those he had said to me as Sarah Kent, when

Lovesong by the Cure came on the radio. The universe seemed to have an agenda. Luke's entire demeanor changed, and whatever he was going to say next went unspoken. He appeared lost in thoughts of another time; a time when he was in love, and life was full of possibilities. It was obvious it had been a long time since he had felt that way.

"Great song," I said, trying to lift the mood.

"Never really been a fan," he replied, "but I knew a girl once who loved this song."

"Yeah? Tell me about her," I said, knowing I was probably pushing more than I should.

He was quiet for a minute or two, and just when I thought he was going to change the subject, he began to tell me the story of the love of his life. He began to tell me about Sarah Kent. He started with how we had met.

"I went to this street dance with my roommate. I thought it was going to be boring." The street dance, the orange wristbands, the country music, and the walk by the horse barn. Our first conversation, first dance, first kiss. . .he remembered it all. The more he talked, the further away he seemed. He was lost in the memories of the girl he loved so many years ago.

For me it was like yesterday. By the time he started describing the trip to the zoo, tears were welling up in my eyes, and I had to bite my lip to stop myself from crying.

"That's when I knew, you know? That day at the zoo. I knew I was going to marry her," he said, looking at the road ahead of us, but clearly seeing another time. Minutes passed before he spoke again. "But life doesn't always turn out like you plan," he finally said.

I knew better than to ask any more questions about his life with Sarah Kent. I had lived that story, and the ending was too tragic to repeat out loud. We didn't talk for the remainder of the drive, with only the reprieve of Skip's snoring to break the silence. Luke pulled up to the parking lot outside my apartment building and offered to walk me inside. I declined, saying I would be fine, and he should get Skip to his new home. I thanked him for bringing me along, saying it was a great day. I meant it. Luke smiled, and drove away.

Back in my apartment, I was grateful my roommate Chloe was gone for the night at her boyfriend's. At least now I could cry in private. And I did. I cried for what felt like hours. I cried for all I had lost, and for the cruelty of the universe dangling it right in front of me now. In the early hours of the morning, I was still awake. I pulled an ice pack from the freezer and placed it over my swollen eyelids. Hearing Luke talk about me in the past tense was brutal. I couldn't sleep and decided to use the time to update my journal. In the past, I had always had to rewrite my entries after the *moment* hit, but now I could upload my entire journal to the Cloud where it could exist indefinitely, much like myself.

I made the password simple, so it would be easy to remember in each life. I opened my laptop, and on it my screensaver read:

> ***Just as a snake sheds its skin,***
> ***We must shed our past over and over again.***
>
> **~ Buddha**

I logged in to my account and typed in "Echo." The screen flashed and filled with hundreds of entries. The most recent was titled "Meeting Luke again." I started a new entry, titling it "Meeting Skip." It was less sad than any of the other titles running through my head. I lived with the pain of losing Luke for so many years, but it was dwarfed by his pain of losing me, especially the way it happened. As I wrote about meeting sweet, lovable Skip, and the wonderful day we had, it occurred to me that telling Luke who I really was would be selfish, bordering on cruel. It was then I decided; I wouldn't tell him. I wouldn't tell him that I was Sarah Kent. I wouldn't remind him of all that we shared and lost. I wouldn't make him relive that terrible day and the sadness that followed. Instead, I would be thankful for the chance to spend time with him, to be near him, hear his laugh, and see his eyes light up when he smiles, but I would never tell him. It would be too selfish, and I couldn't be selfish with him. It took him almost 20 years to let go of the engagement ring he bought me. I couldn't shake the foundation of his world with the knowledge of my continued existence only to leave him again when I turned 23, if not sooner. It broke my heart all over again, but better mine than his. I had all eternity for my heart to mend; I would need it.

CHAPTER 15

CAPA

I spent the entire next day grading papers, catching up from time lost spending the day with Luke and Skip. He hadn't pried too deeply into my language skills, and for that I was grateful. Before meeting Vasily, I didn't realize I knew Russian. Hearing him speak brought it to the surface for me, and it felt as natural as if it were my first language. It had been in another life, but not one that I could remember clearly. I still had visions occasionally, images without names or dates, and in one I wore a large bulky fur parka, fur skin mittens, and boots up to my knees that resembled something worn in an Inuit village. My hair was long and black, and I was walking through a thick snowy forest with a dog. The more I focused, the clearer the vision became. I heard my voice calling to the dog, "*Приходи собака*," as we walked toward a cabin in the distance. The dog ran off, and I heard a woman calling "*Сара, время приходить домой!*" She was telling me to come home, but I didn't want to leave the dog. I chased after him, ducking to avoid the low changing tree branches, laden with heavy snow. The dog ran further into the woods, and soon I lost sight of him. I called out to him again.

"*Приходи собака!*" He was too distracted by whatever scent he was chasing and kept running further away from me. I could still hear him in the distance, but I got turned around. I looked at the ground for my tracks, but in all the running around, tracks were everywhere, in every direction. I cried out for help, but there was no reply, only my voice, echoing in the vast forest.

Sitting in my apartment, I caught a chill remembering my life in the deep wilderness of Russia. I remembered the small village where I lived, and the warm, loving mother who called me "*ангел*," her angel. I remembered losing my way trying to get back home that day, falling into the ravine my mother had told me to avoid so many times before. I remembered hitting my head on a rock after the long fall to the bottom of the ravine and losing consciousness. I woke sometime later, and could hear voices calling my name, searching for the missing teenage girl. I couldn't remember much more about her life, but I certainly remembered her death. My life as Capa Sokolov ended at 17 years old, in a snowy ravine, lost, hurt, cold, and alone.

The memory shook me. It explained the odd birthmark I had on my left temple that looked more like a small scar. It was another remnant of a past life. If I had any doubts before about not telling Luke, they vanished as quickly as the dog running through the woods. I may have infinite lives, but they all end too soon. I couldn't put him through losing me again, which seemed inevitable. If we revived our love story, the ending would be tragic once more, and I couldn't bear the thought of bringing him that kind of pain again.

CHAPTER 16

STARTING OVER

The next morning, I was in no rush to get to class. I found myself in the untenable position of wanting to be close to Luke, yet not wanting to be in the same room with him. I would have given anything to be in his arms but knew that could never happen, so being near him would be just short of torture. Not being near him would be worse, so I was stuck. It wasn't as if I had a choice. I was still his teaching assistant, so attendance was mandatory.

I don't know what to expect when I walked into his classroom, maybe a smile, a wink, something from him that told me he felt something for me. If anything, he seemed indifferent as I entered the room. A quick nod was the only acknowledgment that he even knew I was there. My reaction to his lack of one surprised me. I fumed before he even wrote on the whiteboard. Without even a glance in my direction, he drew large capital letters across the board:

DIVINE INTERVENTION

I didn't mean to be so loud when I laughed at the phrase. It wasn't a soft chuckle, but rather a loud, disapproving guffaw.

"You have a question, Ms. Daley?" Luke asked, looking irritated by my disruption.

"No, sorry Professor Taylor. I was thinking of something else."

"Please try to focus on the topic at hand then," he said, near scolding me. "Let's dive into today's subject matter. Divine intervention. It is a reoccurring theme in ancient Greek literature, classic literary works, as well as modern pieces. Can anyone name one for me?"

"Actually, I do have a question," I interrupted him. "Why are we studying divine intervention? I thought this semester was non-fiction," I said, a bit more rudely than I intended.

"You don't believe in divine intervention, Ms. Daley?" He replied, looking still a bit irritated, but also intrigued.

"Divine intervention implies there is a grand plan. It feeds into the notion of order in the universe where none exists," I said, answering his question. "People believe everything happens for a reason, so they don't have to deal with the stark reality that their existence is random and chaotic. There is no plan, or intervention, divine or otherwise."

Luke didn't reply immediately but instead stared at me for several moments. He was just about to respond, when another student chimed in. Her name was Kristi Nelson, but in my head, I called her "Snooty McWhiner."

"I have to say I disagree. I think you're right Professor Taylor. There totally is divine intervention," Snooty said.

Luke was quiet for a moment, then replied. "I didn't say whether I thought divine intervention was real, I merely asked for an example of a literary work in which it is a featured theme. I appreciate your enthusiasm, Ms. Nelson, but I encourage debate in my classroom."

Snooty appeared disappointed that her effort to gain Luke's favor had fallen flat. I hid my amusement at her failed attempt. He must have

had students vying for his attention often, especially the female ones. He was very attractive after
all, educated, witty, and single. It was bad enough
I wouldn't be with him, but to watch other women
fawn over him was a new level of misery.

"But whether one believes in divine intervention
does not negate the fact that it is a reoccurring theme
in ancient as well as modern literature, and therefore
a part of this class curriculum," he said. "However, I
would be open to discussing this further, Ms. Daley, and any other students who may like to join, of
course, after class today. I will be in the cafeteria at
4:30 for anyone who is interested."

I wasn't sure if that was his way of asking me on
a date. A weird, open invitation kind of date. He
continued with the lesson, but my mind drifted to
other thoughts, like should I meet him after class?
Even if we couldn't be a couple again, perhaps we
could be friends. We obviously enjoyed each other's
company, and it would be a way for me to still have
some connection with him. A little Luke was better than no Luke at all. I decided I would be in the
cafeteria at 4:30.

CHAPTER 17

FRIENDS

I went back to my apartment to debate with myself. I knew spending time with Luke would only make me want to tell him, but I already decided that was both foolish and unkind. If he didn't believe me, I would end up in a padded white room, and if he did, he could end up losing me all over again in a few short years. I could use this time to wean myself off of Luke. I could spend time with him now, and maybe find out he's a different person, not the same Luke that I was pulled from all too soon. I would get over him and still have him as my friend. That was my plan. Unfortunately, my lives rarely went according to plan. *Why start now?* I asked myself.

I changed out of my baggy grey sweatpants and looked through my painfully small apartment closet for something to wear. I wrestled with the hangers, crammed in so tight that everything was always just a little bit wrinkled. I pushed past the collection of UMD T-shirts I'd gathered since my admission to the college, past the limited selection of interview blouses and blazers, and landed briefly on a yellow sundress. It wasn't exactly like the one I wore that day 20 years ago. I don't know if Luke had even known that I had worn it that day in the bank. It was his favorite, but I wasn't sure if he had seen me in it afterwards, huge red blood stain and all. Something pulled at me to put on the dress. It was deep down in my gut. I have never been very good about following my gut. *Why start now?* I wondered.

I arrived at 4:35 at the school cafeteria, wearing jeans and a T-shirt with UMD emblazoned across the front, over the image of the school mascot, Champ the bulldog. I saw Luke sitting over by the window. I must have stared at him for five minutes before he looked my way. I wished I could have looked at him longer. I waved, motioning to the soda dispenser, signaling him that I would be right over after I grabbed a drink. I pulled a glass out of the rack, pushed it against the lever for a diet Coke, and filled my glass to the brim. I realized I had forgotten to put ice in first and poured a bit out to make room. I pushed the glass against the ice lever, but nothing happened. I pushed again, and still no ice. I tried a third time and then the machine churned, erupting ice not only into my glass, but overflowing all over the floor. Meanwhile, Luke watched from the window seat. For a moment I was lost, thinking of the time Luke and I had been together, getting ready for our favorite of evenings, movie night.

"Grab me a pop while you're out there," Luke called from the living room.

"Grab me a pop, please, you mean," I replied, laughing. "You need to ask nicely if you expect me to do things for you."

"Grab me a pop, please, my beautiful darling, my angel, love of my life," he called back to me.

"Much better," I replied. "You are a very smart man, Luke Taylor. You should be a teacher or something."

I was still holding my glass against the ice dispenser when the custodian yelled.

"Back up from the pop machine!" His voice shook me from my memory of Luke and me, only to find Luke looking at me, but not really at me. Not at Sarah

Kent, the version of me that he loved. I jerked my hand away from the stream of ice and apologized profusely to the custodian.

"I'm so, so sorry," I stammered. "I didn't mean to make such a mess. Please let me help you clean it up."

"You've done enough, young lady," he scolded, "Now just get out of my way and let me deal with this mess you made before someone slips and breaks their neck!"

"Again, I'm so sorry," I said, moving away from the ice cubes all over the cafeteria floor. I looked in Luke's direction, and saw him with his head down, and shoulders visibly shaking with laughter. I walked over to him anyway.

"So, you saw all that, did you?" I asked, already knowing the answer. He was laughing so hard he couldn't catch his breath to reply.

"Alright, that's enough. I get it. You always did like slapstick," I said. I caught my breath the second after I said it.

"Oh, come on, you can't blame me. That was hilarious. Wait, what? What do you mean? How did you know I like slapstick?" Luke asked.

"Um, I just assumed it. Don't all men like slap-stick?" I replied, trying to bluff my way out of the awkward slip.

Luke stared at me for a moment, then said, "I can't speak for all men, but yes, I do enjoy the classic form of comedy known as slapstick. I make no apology for my love of The Three Stooges." His eyes sparkled as he continued to chuckle lightly at my expense. I didn't mind.

AMY LARSON MARBLE

CHAPTER 18

DÉJÀ VU ALL OVER AGAIN

Once Luke regained his composure, I asked him how Skip was adjusting to his new home.

"He's great," he replied. "I didn't realize how quiet my house was before I got him. Thanks, by the way, for going with me to pick him up. That was very kind of you."

"Yeah, it was no problem. I was glad to do it. He's a great dog. I imagine he's good company," I said.

"Yeah, the best really. I'd gotten so used to being on my own, I didn't realize how lonely my place was. . .how lonely I was, really," he said, apparently without meaning to, because he quickly changed the topic. "You don't believe in divine intervention then?" He asked rather abruptly.

"Should we wait for the other students to join us before diving into that one?" I asked, hoping to avoid the topic all together. If I had to debate why I didn't believe in it, I would have to provide my reasoning, which would be hard to do without revealing my unique style of existence.

"I doubt anyone else will actually show up. I was a little surprised to see you to be honest. You seemed uncomfortable with the subject today in class," Luke said with a curious smile.

I sat silently for a moment, pondering what to say next. Everything that came to mind started with a past life and ended the way it always ended; me, dead before my 24th birthday. I was just about to speak when Luke interrupted.

"I'm really glad you came, because I have something I want to ask you. I was hoping on Friday, if you're free that is, if you wouldn't mind watching Skip for the evening?"

"Sure," I replied. "I'd be glad to. I have some papers to grade, but I could bring those along. What time would you like me to be there?"

"Thank you, I appreciate it very much. Skip seems to really like you and I just don't feel right leaving him home alone all night. Would 6:30 work? I'm sup-posed to meet my date at 7:00," Luke replied.

I felt like someone punched me in the stomach. Of course, he would be dating. He said he was finally moving on. He was selling the engagement ring, so it made perfect sense that he would be dating. I would have to accept that Luke had a life outside of me, in-cluding a social life.

I must have been in my own thoughts for too long, because Luke asked me again.

"If you're busy though, I wouldn't want to impose," he said.

"No, it's not an imposition. I would love to hang with Skip. I'll be at your place at 6:30," I said, stand-ing up from the table. I suddenly didn't feel like talking anymore.

AMY LARSON MARBLE

CHAPTER 19

MOVING ON

I spent the rest of the week fuming, and Friday arrived all too quickly. I considered canceling, but I decided it wasn't Skip's fault, and I did really like that dog, so at 6:30 I found myself outside Luke's house. I took three deep breaths and knocked on the door.

"Come in," Luke yelled from inside, "the door is unlocked."

I walked inside and was greeted by Skip almost immediately. He pushed his head into my hand, and wagged his tail so quickly he nearly knocked over a glass on the coffee table. I looked around again at the living room. It looked the same as the last time I was here; clean, everything in its place. Somehow it looked different knowing now that it would never be our home together.

Luke walked out from the bedroom, wearing a dark grey suit, crisp white shirt and silver-tone tie. He clearly spent a significant amount of time on his hair. He was dressed for his date, one that he must have been hoping to impress. It was only 6:40 when there was another knock at the door. Luke's date had arrived early. Luke rushed over to the door, glanced over his shoulder at me with an expression that could only be described as anxious, and in walked his date, Shannon.

Shannon Johnson was a professor at UMD as well, and not only was she brilliant, she was also incredibly beautiful. I guess it had been too much to hope for that she would have an eye patch, or gout or something. Luke gave me a list of instructions on where to find Skip's food, how much to give him, his favorite treats, and what time to let him out before he went to bed. I nodded politely, fairly confident in my ability to watch a dog for a few hours, but let him go through the list anyway.

Luke and Shannon walked out the door, laughing over something Luke said as they left, but it was too quiet for me to hear. Skip started to whine as they walked down the sidewalk toward his car.

"I don't like it either, buddy, but we want him to be happy," I said, scratching Skip's ears. "How about we drown our sorrows? Popcorn for me and kibble for you."

I turned on Netflix, surfed through the movie selections, and without meaning to, landed on *Say Anything.* I considered watching it, but decided it was just too sad, possibly pathetic, for me to watch that particular movie with Luke's dog while Luke was out with another woman. He was back out in the dating world. I should be too. *Yeah right,* I thought.

After his date with Shannon, Luke came home and offered to walk me back to my apartment. It was only three blocks away, and I told him I would be fine, but he insisted. We had only been walking for a couple of minutes, and I was just about to ask him about his date, when a kid came racing by on a bike, and almost knocked me over.

"Hey! Watch where you're going," Luke yelled at him.

The words were barely out of his mouth before the boy careened off the path and wiped out in the trees. He flew off his bike, and landed with a sickening thud, followed immediately by a terrible scream of pain. We ran to him as fast as we could. He was lying there, his torso crumpled over his legs, and his screams turned to a whimpering cry.

He was shaking, and his leg was covered in blood. I knelt beside him and saw the branch that was sticking out of his thigh. It was about the diameter of a dime and was lodged deep in the boy's leg. I told Luke to call 911 and began to assess the situation. My initial triage determined the branch had missed the femoral artery, but if I didn't stabilize his leg immediately, that could change quickly. The boy was writhing in pain, and I was concerned he would exacerbate his injury if he kept moving his leg. I needed a way to stabilize the impaled limb while we waited for the ambulance to arrive. I asked Luke to throw me my backpack and took out a scarf I kept with me for bad hair days.

I wrapped the scarf around the boy's leg, crisscrossing it to immobilize the stick as much as possible. Next I examined him for signs of shock. His skin color appeared normal, but his skin was clammy to the touch. His breathing seemed regular, but I was still concerned. I turned on my iPhone flashlight to check his eyes.

"Pupils are reacting normally," I said aloud. "How are you feeling?" I asked the boy. "Any nausea? Are you dizzy at all?"

He replied that his head hurt, but he wasn't dizzy. He had most likely hit his head in the crash as well. I would have to let the EMTs know when they arrived. I was busy tending to the boy's injuries, but I could still see the look on Luke's face from the corner of my eye.

"Were you pre-med before you became my teaching assistant?" he asked, the tone of his voice somewhere between disbelief and admiration.

The ambulance arrived, and as I turned away from its flashing red lights, my vision blurred into images of a field in the distance. The field was filled with the bodies of soldiers; some wounded, others dying. Off in the distance I heard bombs exploding. They were far enough away that we were safe, but close enough that it made me wince. I looked down at my hands; they were covered with blood. I wrapped the tourniquet around the young soldier's calf, just beneath the kneecap. The gash was deep, and bleeding uncontrollably. I applied pressure to the wound, but the shrapnel was still buried deep in his leg. The soldier screamed, begging me to make the pain stop. "Please don't let them take my leg, nurse, please!" He passed out from the pain before I made any promises I couldn't keep. I kept the pressure on the wound as the medics lifted his gurney and carried him to the surgical tent. I walked out of the tent, grateful to step away from the pain and suffering, if only for a minute or two. The breeze blew my hair into my face, sticking to the half-dried blood on my cheek.

I walked down towards the river, passing the fresh graves of the soldiers, marked only by broken boards stuck in the dirt, names hastily written across them. The flapping of the Union flag was the last thing I heard before an artillery shell exploded a few feet from where I was standing. My life as Sara Barnes ended at 23 years old, drenched in blood and surrounded by anguish.

CHAPTER 20

SECOND IMPRESSIONS

The paramedics loaded the boy into the ambulance, the branch limb still secured by my scarf around his leg. "You did a nice job, miss," one of the EMTs said as they lifted him into the back of the ambulance.

"Thanks," I said. "Will he be alright?" The EMT nodded yes as they closed the doors. Luke was quiet for a moment, and then asked me "What is it about you?"

"That's a bit cryptic. What do you mean?" I replied, knowing full well the confusion he was facing. It had been the same look he had given me when I passed him on the horse trail on our second date, when I was Sarah Kent, when we were falling in love.

"I can't put my finger on it, but being with you feels. . . strangely familiar," he said. "Like I've known you longer than I have."

"Well, that's less cryptic," I said sarcastically, not wanting to give in to the desire to tell him who I really was. I didn't say anything more, unable to trust I wouldn't become a rambling idiot, spilling all the reincarnation beans. Instead I changed the subject.

"I should get back to my apartment. Chloe will be wondering where I am." I lied, knowing even if Chloe were home, she never kept track of my whereabouts.

"Okay, at least let me walk you the rest of the way," Luke said, gesturing with his hand in the direction of Junction Apartments at the end of campus.

"Sure, that would be nice, thanks," I replied, relieved he had moved on from questioning me about my medical expertise. "I need to finish grading those papers anyway."

"Why don't I take the rest of the papers home with me too," Luke asked. "It's the least I can do to thank you for hanging with Skip tonight. I insist."

I wasn't really in the mood to grade papers, so I agreed. I asked Luke if he wanted to come up to my apartment, and I would get him the short stack that remained. We walked up to the third floor and went inside.

"Nice place," he said, looking around.

"Thanks. There's not much we can do about the wall color, but we've done our best to make it comfortable," I said. "I have the essays in my room. I'll be right back. Make yourself at home."

Luke looked around the small apartment while I was gathering the papers and called out to me from the living room.

"I've seen this painting somewhere before. Is this yours?" He asked.

I walked out of my bedroom, my arms cradling the stack of papers. Luke was pointing to the framed print I had of a Leonid Afremov painting. It was called *Unexpected Meeting*. It had been on exhibit at the Minneapolis Institute of Art in 1998 when Luke and Sarah Kent spent the afternoon at the museum. It was my favorite piece in the exhibit, and the print was a gift from my mom when I moved to this apartment.

"Yeah, it's a Leonid Afremov," I said. Before I could say more, Luke interrupted.

"*Unexpected Meeting,* yeah, I know," he said. "I saw it at MIA when I lived in Minneapolis.

I didn't know what to say that wouldn't lead to more questions, so I changed the subject, handing him the remaining papers.

"You sure about grading the rest of these? I don't mind doing it. It's not like I have anything else going on this weekend," I said.

Luke continued to stare at the print, his eyes looking beyond the painting to another time; a time when he was with Sarah Kent, the love of his life.

"I'm sure," he finally said. "I could use the distraction." He left without saying more, and I watched him from my window as he walked across the parking lot into the darkness.

CHAPTER 21

ALWAYS SOMETHING THERE TO REMIND ME

The next morning, I walked to the campus cafeteria to get some breakfast after discovering my stockpile of Cheerios was low and Chloe had eaten the last of my frozen waffles. The cafeteria had a decent selection of breakfast choices, but I headed straight for the waffle station, as usual. My mind drifted back to the last time I ate waffles with Luke at Al's Breakfast in Minneapolis. The beeping of the waffle alarm quickly brought me back to the present day, the one where I'm not Sarah Kent, and I don't live in Minneapolis, and where Luke is dating other women. I lost my appetite.

The line of people behind me waiting for the waffle iron began to grumble, so I took my breakfast anyway and looked for a place to sit. A seat by the window opened, so I hurried over and sat down before anyone else could take it. I stared out the window and tried desperately to think of something other than Luke.

I brought my mail with me to read over breakfast, and in the stack of envelopes was a bright pink announcement card. Professor Briggs and his wife Debra had their baby. On the front of the card was a picture of a beautiful little baby girl, with a mop of dark brown hair and a small polka dot bow holding her bangs away from her face. On the back was a picture of the new parents, both looking extremely tired, but very happy. I looked up from the postcard just as Luke walked in the cafeteria. So much for trying to not think about him.

Luke walked over to my table, flashed that ridiculously amazing smile of his, and said, "Hey you. You must have quite the appetite after all the excitement last night."

"What? What excitement? Oh, that's right, the boy on the bike. Any word on his condition?" I asked.

"Yeah, I called the hospital this morning. They said he will be fine. The nurse said whoever provided first aid at the scene probably saved his life. Apparently, the injury to his leg was extremely close to the artery. If you hadn't secured the branch so well, he could have been in real trouble. Nicely done Miss Daley," he said.

"Thanks, but it wasn't that big of a deal," I replied. "I'm just glad he'll be okay."

"Yes, he will, which is more than I can say for that waffle. Are you seriously dipping that in your orange juice?" Luke asked, with a mildly disgusted look on his face.

I hadn't even noticed that I had been waffle dipping while talking with Luke.

"I have a highly refined palate," I said, more as a reflex than an intended response.

My reply caught him off guard. Luke took a visible quick breath in, stared at me, but said nothing in reply. I wanted to kick myself. I knew he would be reminded of Sarah Kent when I said it. I didn't mean to drudge up memories for him. It was a selfish moment of weakness. I resolved to not let it happen again. I changed the subject in the most painful way possible. I asked him about his date.

"With all the commotion last night, I forgot to ask you how your date went," I asked, cringing inside and hoping he would tell me it wasn't any of my business.

"Um, fine, I think," he answered, the look on his face clearly puzzled by the change in topic. "I am seeing her again tomorrow night. That's actually why I came over here. I was hoping you wouldn't mind hanging with Skip again at my place."

Great. Date number two. So glad I can help facilitate your love life, I thought to myself. I was about to agree to do it anyway, when I remembered I had promised Chloe I would pick up her brother from the airport tomorrow night. Finally, the universe was cutting me some slack. It was a bit sad to be grateful for an airport run, but I was.

"I'm sorry, I can't tomorrow. I promised to help my roommate with something. Any other time though, I would be glad to. I love that dog," I replied.

Luke gave a faint smile and told me not to worry about it. Skip would survive a short time at home alone. He would have to get used to it eventually anyway.

"I can't have you at my beck and call whenever, right?" Luke's comment came off as awkward, and more familiar than a professor and student should be. He immediately retracted it. "I didn't mean it that way, I just meant Skip really likes when you're there."

"It's okay, I knew what you meant. I like it too," I said, knowing I meant more than that. I took a breath to find my resolve, dipping the last of my waffle in my glass of juice. "So, I'll see you in class on Monday," I said, ending the conversation. Luke looked a bit taken back. He replied he'd see me then and walked away toward the cafeteria door. I watched him walk out, biting my lip to keep from calling out to him that I changed my mind, and would gladly be at his beck and call.

CHAPTER 22

RESIGNATION

I went back to my apartment, sulked for a bit, and then decided I would spend the day with friends. I didn't know how much time I would have left in this life as Sarah Daley, but it seemed wasteful to spend the rest of it pining away for something or someone I couldn't have. Chloe was already gone for the weekend with her parents, and I didn't have many other friends, so I called my mom and asked her to lunch.

"To what do I owe the honor?" she joked, responding to my request for a lunch date.

"I don't need a reason to spend time with my mom," I replied. "I just thought we could hang."

"You don't need a reason, no, but you usually have one. Is everything okay, sweetheart?" she asked.

I lied and told her everything was fine, and I just wanted to see her. She played along, knowing I was upset about something. She replied she would love to spend some time with me. She suggested we meet at Va Bene Caffe on East Superior Street. It sat right on the lake and the food was always delicious. My mom knew how to take my mind off my troubles, even if I didn't tell her what my troubles were.

She arrived before me and had gotten us a table in the open-air grotto section of the restaurant. It was a wonderful spot. The fresh lake air, cool breeze, watching the seagulls flying overhead, all while enjoying the bruschetta and honey goat cheese with pears from the antipasto menu. That was normally what I would do. Now I just picked at my food, moving the fork around the plate. My mom noticed and asked me what was wrong.

"Are you feeling okay, sweetheart? You usually love the food here. If I didn't know better, I would say you're nursing a broken heart," she said as she took my hand in hers.

I didn't know what to say. As far as my parents knew, I had never had a boyfriend, much less been in love. I struggled to find a cover story, something to ease her mind that I was going to be okay, even if I couldn't hide my current state.

"I think I'm nervous about graduation. I don't know what I want to do with my degree, and I've worked so hard to do well in school, and now it will all be over soon, and I'm just feeling a bit lost, I guess," I said, hoping I had thrown in enough reasonable insecurities to deflect her mom spider-sense from detecting heartbreak.

She looked at me for a long moment, then said "Okay, if that's what you say is bothering you, we'll go with that. Sarah, you are smart, funny and endlessly talented. I have no doubt you have an amazing life in front of you. If you find yourself doubting it, I want you to take three long deep breaths, and remind yourself of all you've accomplished."

That was my mom's go-to move whenever she was stressed. She said three long deep breaths was the difference between making a rash decision or a reasoned choice. That is exactly what I had done. I had made the reasoned choice to not tell Luke who I was, to not be with him and to let him move on. Now I just needed to have my heart get on board with the reasoned choice my head had made. My mom was still holding my hand, and I managed to hold back my tears.

"Thanks mom. I promise I will. I love you," I said, feeling terrible I couldn't tell her anything about Luke or my life as Sarah Kent. All the people I loved didn't know the truth about me, and because I loved them, I could never tell them.

We left the restaurant and took a walk along the shore before saying goodbye for the night. My mom dropped me off at my apartment and I binge-watched episodes of *Friends* until I fell asleep. Sunday morning arrived as if the universe hadn't realized I had given up all hope of being reunited with the love of my life.

CHAPTER 23

DISTRACTIONS

I moped around the apartment, wishing I had agreed to watch Skip tonight. At least then I could focus on something other than all the lives ahead of me without Luke. I did still have to meet Chloe's brother, Aaron, at the airport tonight, but I could have managed that and still watched Skip. I just didn't want to be a part of Luke's second date with Shannon in any way. After two loads of laundry, I cleaned the kitchen, vacuumed the entire apartment, and set up the bed linens for Chloe's brother who would be staying with us for the next week.

Chloe was at work all night and asked me to take her car to pick up Aaron at 9:30, which left me more than an hour before I would have to leave. The apartment was spotless, and I had binged all the Ross and

Rachel I could for one night, so I decided to go for a quick run. I found my favorite running socks, put on my ID bracelet, grabbed my iPod and started down my favorite path towards the park.

I found my stride just as *Mr. Blue Sky* came on my iPod. The path led to a great lookout spot, up the hill high enough so I could see all the way to the lake. I reached the top and took three long deep breaths. On the third exhale, I turned to start back down the trail when I saw him. Luke. Only it wasn't just Luke. It was Luke on his second date with Shannon. They were on a romantic walk through the park and headed directly towards me. I darted behind a line of pine trees, and doubled back the way I came, hoping I could avoid them all together.

I went off the path to take a shortcut back, turning up the volume on my iPod to distract me from the near miss with Luke and his date in the park. Billie Eilish sang *Bad Guy*, and I picked up the pace. Suddenly I felt a push from behind. It didn't knock me to the ground, but the second hit did. I fell hard, face first onto a large rock. I looked up, wiping the blood from my split lip, and there were two men towering over me. The bigger one leered at me, making my stomach instantly tighten. His eyes were bloodshot, and his speech slurred.

"Quick, grab her feet," he said to his accomplice. "Before she tries to run."

The smaller one looked a little scared, like he didn't want to be there.

"I don't know man, maybe we should just go," he pleaded. "There's too many people in the park. Someone will see us."

I was just about to scream, but instead, something inside me snapped. I took all the frustration, anger and sadness that had been welling up inside me for days and channeled it into a focused kick to the big one's left knee. He crumpled to the ground, and screamed in pain. The other guy stood there, not knowing what to do. I leapt to my feet. From the ground the big one yelled at him to take me down. He lunged at me, but I slipped my shoulder back to the side, and he fell forward, missing me completely. As soon as he landed on the ground, I took the opportunity to slam my foot onto his ankle as hard as I could, and dislocated it from his leg. The big one was back on his feet, limping, but angry. He took out a knife from his waistband and began waving it at me.

"You're going to pay for that, bitch," he snarled at me, while his accomplice continued writhing in pain on the ground.

I waited a moment to read his body position, watching his midsection for clues to his next move. He lunged at me and in the same moment, I quickly moved in closer, blocked his arm with my left forearm, and used it to lever the knife out of his hand. I came at him with my right elbow for an upward blow to his chin. Before he fell over backwards to the ground, I wrapped my right arm around his neck, pulling his head down as I drove my knee into his groin, ensuring he wouldn't be able to chase after me.

I stood for a moment to catch my breath when I heard footsteps running up the path behind me. I prepared myself for more attackers. I stood ready to fight, when a small crowd descended upon the scene. In the front were Luke and Shannon. Luke ran over to me, while instructing his date to call the police.

"Sarah! Are you okay? Are you hurt?" Luke asked, with the same panic I had heard in his voice once before.

"It's alright Luke. I'm fine. They didn't hurt me."

"Are you sure? Are you bleeding? Is that your blood?" Luke asked worriedly.

"Yeah, I guess it is. He got my arm a little with his knife," I replied.

Before Luke or I could say anything more, the police arrived. One of the officers took my statement, while the others handcuffed my assailants and took them away in their squad cars. Luke insisted the officer call an ambulance, but I told him I was fine. The officer said he had been a medic in the army and asked to look at my arm. After a brief examination of the cut, he said it could have used some stitches, but if I didn't mind having a scar, he could seal it up right there with some medical glue and tape. He went to his squad car to get his medical kit and told us to wait on the park bench.

Luke's face was nearly drained of color. I thought he might faint and asked him if he was okay.

"Am I okay? Are you kidding me right now?" he said, the volume of his voice loud enough to draw the attention of his date, who had been sitting on the park bench across from us while Luke was by my side. "This is crazy, it's just like before. I've said the same things, seen the same things, but it's not possible. It's crazy."

"Luke, you're not making much sense right now. You should go back to your date. I'll be fine. The officer will patch me up and give me a ride home," I said, knowing full well he was making perfect sense. "Besides, I still have to get to the airport to pick up Chloe's brother."

"You can't go to the airport after this. I'll go. I'll take Shannon home, and I'll pick up Chloe's brother," Luke insisted.

"You don't even know what he looks like," I said. "I'm fine. Really, what's one more scar, right?" I said, making a sad attempt to lighten the moment.

"I'm taking Shannon home, and then I will pick you up to go to the airport. Have the officer drive you home, and I will be at your apartment soon. No argument," he said and walked away, leaving no opportunity for further discussion on the matter.

"Fine," I said, "but bring Skip along."

The whole way home I couldn't help to think about the last time Luke had seen me in a fight. He must have been thinking about it too as he drove Shannon home. The similarities would be too much for him to dismiss as coincidence, but he wouldn't have any other reasonable explanation for it. Tonight had been so much like that night in front of First Avenue in Minneapolis. He had said practically the same words to me then.

I was glad he would have time to think things over before picking me up. His rational mind would find a way to justify the feeling of déjà vu. Perhaps as nothing more than a sad testament to the frequency of violence in our society. At least that is what I hoped he would conclude.

CHAPTER 24

LUKE'S MOMENT

Luke showed up at my apartment shortly after the police brought me home. They passed in the hallway, and I overheard the officer say to Luke "That girl sure can fight. Those guys didn't know who they were messing with."

"That's for sure. Thank you so much for bringing her home, Officer," Luke replied, and continued to my door.

"Ready to go?" he asked, the concern still showing on his face.

"Yeah, just let me grab my keys," I replied, and picked up my keychain from the kitchen counter.

We walked to his car in silence, the awkward tension as thick as the fog that rolled off the lake in the morning. The drive to the airport was thankfully short, and soon we were inside the terminal, still not having spoken more than a word or two. It wasn't until the announcement that Flight 2183 from Chicago was delayed that Luke broke the silence.

"Looks like we have some time to kill. Should we wait it out at the Tap House?" he asked.

"Sure, sounds good," I replied, grateful for the break from the uncomfortable silence. "I would offer to buy you a beer, but you know, the whole being a minor thing gets in the way," I said, attempting to lighten the mood.

Luke feigned a brief smile, and we walked toward the airport's restaurant and bar. The sign at the hostess podium directed patrons to seat themselves, and Luke pointed to a table towards the back of the restaurant, away from the televisions and crowded bar section.

"You know you don't have to stay here. Aaron and I could catch an Uber to my apartment," I said as soon as we sat down.

"No, I'm glad his flight is delayed. I have to talk to you about something, and there's no time like the present," he said, his face dead serious.

"No kidding," I said under my breath, but not quietly enough. Luke ignored my remark and began talking to me as if we were in his classroom, filled with dozens of students seated for a lecture.

"Here are the facts as I see them," he began his speech. "The day we drove to pick up Skip, I told you about the girl I was planning to ask to marry me. Her name was Sarah Kent. Now, for some inexplicable reason, everything about you reminds me of her. But it's more than that. You are so much like her, it's uncanny. I feel like I'm going crazy. If it were just the physical resemblance, or that you like the same music, or even how you like to dunk your waffles in orange juice, I could write it off as coincidence. I have tried to do that. But then tonight, when you were fighting those assholes in the park, even the way you move is like her. You even have the same scars."

He grabbed my left hand and looked at the red mark on my palm, just below my thumb. What was a birthmark in this life had once been a scar on Sarah Kent's hand from a bowl of hot melted butter made for movie night popcorn. Luke had noticed it when he took my hand the night of the street dance when we met, and apparently it had caught his eye tonight.

"Am I crazy," he pleaded, his voice trembling, "because I feel like I'm losing my mind. Tell me if I'm crazy."

Just like that, all my strength was gone. My resolve to keep the truth from Luke faded to a faint echo in the distance, warning me not to do it.

"I can't," I replied in a near whisper. "I can't tell you you're crazy, because you're not. There's a reason I am so much like Sarah Kent. It's the same reason I know your favorite ice cream is mint chocolate chip. It's why I know you ripped your jean jacket on the nail sticking out of the fence at the horse ranch with the big black dog named Skip.

It's why I know you don't like The Cure but agreed to go see them at First Avenue anyway. It's why I have wished a million times since then that I had never set foot in that bank. If I could turn back time, I would have walked into Al's breakfast and we would have spent the morning together, and maybe even the rest of our lives." I took a breath. I had been talking so quickly I had forgotten to breathe.

Luke looked completely shell-shocked. His eyes were wider than I had ever seen them, and his mouth was open, as if he was about to say something, but nothing came out.

"The ring was really beautiful by the way," I said quietly, looking at my hand without meaning to.

"Sarah? Is it really you?" he finally spoke, quietly, as if the words were too absurd to be said aloud. "How is that possible? I don't understand."

"That is the million-dollar question," I answered. "Truth is, I don't know. All I know is I have lived several lives, and my last one was as Sarah Kent."

AMY LARSON MARBLE

CHAPTER 25

REVELATIONS

What had been a delayed flight turned into a canceled one, so Luke and I went back to my apartment for the night. We talked for hours about our past, my search for answers, my scars from past lives, as well as my skills.

"So, the fighting, the horseback riding, and the Russian? That was all stuff from your past lives?" he asked, his eyes wide as he took in the incredible story of my existence. "What else can you do? Was that the field medic stuff too, with the kid on the bike?"

"Yeah, all of it, and in each life, I'm named Sarah. How's that for weird? I was Capa once, but that's just Sarah in Russian." I told him what I had coined as psychic muscle memory, and how the skills emerged when I needed them.

"I'm really good at knitting too," I said, trying to lighten the mood.

"Well now you're just bragging," he replied, trying to joke along, but his voice was still shaking. I could see the stunned look in his eyes and thought maybe if he could see my lives in writing, it would be easier to get a handle on our unique situation.

I told him about my journal. I opened my laptop and clicked on my Dropbox account. The entries detailed each of my lives, as well as each death. It was then Luke noticed the disturbing pattern that had plagued me as long as I could remember. It was time for full disclosure.

"Now you know. I live over and over again, but never past 23. I don't know how much longer I'll be Sarah Daley before I get ripped away from this life and tossed into the next," I said, closing my laptop.

Overwhelmed from the evening's revelations, we laid on the floor, and stared up at my ceiling. There was so much more to be said, but nothing we could say would change the past or the future. Finally, exhaustion overtook us. When we woke, it was morning, and I was resting my head on his shoulder, just like I used to.

"Now what," Luke asked, still laying on the floor. "Where do we go from here?"

"I don't know," I said. "It wouldn't be fair to either one of us to pick up where we left off when I may only have a few years left in this life."

Luke took a deep breath and stood up. He reached his hand out to me and pulled me up to him. He put his hands on either side of my face, staring at me as if still in disbelief.

"The fact is Sarah, you don't know when you'll leave this life and neither do I. What I do know is this. Whether it's one year or one day, I don't want to go another moment without you. I've waited 20 years; I can't wait another 20 seconds."

He pulled me to him and kissed me. It wasn't a first kiss. It was the kiss of soulmates, separated by years of sadness and longing, finally reunited. The apartment with the unsightly walls and ugly carpet suddenly became the most romantic place in the world.

CHAPTER 26

THE WEDDING

It was a small ceremony, held in Grand Marais on the North Shore of Lake Superior. We invited our families and just a few close friends. Luke's parents weren't thrilled with him marrying a student, but they took to me quickly. It helped that I knew so much about them already. My parents thought Luke was too old for me, but my mom said she always knew I was an old soul, and Luke was kind, so she helped me win over my dad. We invited Pam Hadley, who came with her husband and two kids.

After the reception, I asked her to take a walk by the water with me. I told her everything and apologized for not reaching out sooner. After I answered about a hundred questions to prove I was who I said I was, Pam hugged me so tight I could hardly breathe.

I talked to her about my many lives, my abilities, and mostly my fear of leaving again.

"Just because you can't recall any lives that lasted longer than 24 years, doesn't mean you haven't lived one. Or that this one won't last longer. You said yourself there are lives you don't fully remember, just visions and distant memories," she said.

"Now I remember why you're my best friend. You always know the right thing to say," I replied, and hugged her again, even tighter than before.

"We've got bigger problems," Pam said, looking at me. "How am I going to hang out with my best friend who's 20 years younger than me without looking like I'm having a mid-life crisis?"

We burst out laughing. The kind of laugh only best friends share. I hadn't laughed like that in 20 years.

CHAPTER 27

GREECE

After a long and wonderful flight, we landed in Athens. We dropped our luggage at the Royal Olympic Hotel, and set out to see the city. As we walked down the cobbled streets, Luke asked me if anything looked familiar.

"And don't say anything about Petros bringing you a glass of wine," he joked.

"No, I think this may be a first," I replied.

I leaned over to kiss him for the first time on our honeymoon. It was the first of many. I didn't know how much longer I would be Sarah Daley, but I didn't dwell on it. I was happier in that moment than in any of my lives, and it felt enough to last an eternity.

We strolled through the cobblestone streets, and I pulled Luke into a small shop filled with glassworks.

I spotted a small, delicate glass sculpture of a dolphin. The artist had mounted the fragile creation on a mantle of wave-shaped glass, so the dolphin appeared to be leaping from the water. It felt joyous and triumphant. I was just about to ask Luke if we should buy it when I noticed an elderly gentleman staring at me from the doorway. He was standing there, mesmerized. There was something familiar about him, something about his eyes. I found myself staring back. Our eyes locked, and he reached his hand to his chest, not in distress, but as if he were startled. I walked over to him, drawn to him in a way I could not explain.

"Excuse me, do I know you?" I asked the man *Me synchoreís, se xéro,* trying my best not to mutilate the beautiful Greek language.

Eísai esý! Eísai esý, he kept repeating "it's you, it's you!" His eyes were wide with disbelief.

"Please stay here, I'll be right back," I said to him and turned to find Luke. He was at the counter, buying the dolphin statue that had drawn me into the store. I told him about the strange encounter with the elderly man and asked him to come with me to talk to him. Luke paid the cashier, and took the small beautiful bag containing the glass sculpture. I pleaded with him to hurry, wanting to find out what the man meant by his exclamation.

"Please hurry, Luke, I don't want him to leave," I said.

I pulled him by the arm and led him to the store front, but we were too late. The old man had gone.

"He couldn't have gotten too far. Let's look around," I said to Luke, still pulling on his arm.

"Do we have to? I'm starving, and we haven't even unpacked our luggage yet. Let's go back to the hotel, take a long, hot shower, get dressed up and go eat a ridiculously expensive meal," he replied, and gave me the look that he knew made me melt.

"Fine," I sighed. "But if he was about to tell me that I'm a long-lost heir to an enormous fortune, that's on you."

"It's a risk I'm willing to take if it means we can get something to eat," he replied.

It was a brief walk back to the hotel, and when we got to our room, Luke insisted I take the first shower.

"You know you need longer than I do to get ready. Just leave me some hot water," he said.

"Just leave me some hot water, please, you mean," I said.

"Leave me some hot water, please, my beautiful darling, my angel, love of my life," he called back to me.

"You remembered," I replied. "You are a very smart man, Luke Taylor. It's a good thing you're a teacher."

Our eyes met, both of us smiling at the repeated moment from our previous lives as Luke Taylor and Sarah Kent. I blew him a kiss, then stepped into the hot streaming water flowing from the rainfall showerhead. The bathroom featured an exquisite marble shower stall. It was the most luxurious hotel I had ever seen. I quickly washed my hair, not knowing how long would be too long to keep my promise of saving some hot water for Luke. My stomach was growling, and I was looking forward to a fabulous meal at the rooftop restaurant with views of the Acropolis and Parthenon. Still, I found myself preoccupied with thoughts of the old man at the glass shop. The way he had looked me, like he was seeing a ghost. I wished we had been able to speak with him. It felt unfinished, and a bit unsettling. I started to shave my legs when I heard Luke say something from the other room.

"Sorry, can't hear you. I'll be out soon, I promise," I yelled from the shower.

The door opened, cold air rushing through the bathroom. Luke stood there, his mouth hanging open, as if the words were stuck in his throat.

"Sarah, you need to read this. You need to read this now," he said, holding a piece of hotel stationary in his hand.

AMY LARSON MARBLE

CHAPTER 28

GHOSTS OF ATHENS PAST

I grabbed a towel for my hair, wrapped it around my head, and draped the thick hotel bathrobe around my shoulders, cinching the waist tight while drying my hands enough to take the letter from Luke.

Luke was pale, and hadn't said another word since handing me the letter.

"You've already read it? What does it say?" I asked him.

"Just read it," he said.

I unfolded the paper, holding my breath.

Dearest Sarah,
I apologize for my hasty departure from the store front today. I was too stunned at the time to say

the words you need to hear. I followed you back to your hotel, and leave you this letter as a warning. You told me once long ago that this day may come, and if it did, I would have to be brave. I failed in that endeavor this morning, and for that I ask your forgiveness. You always told me a mistake is only a mistake if you repeat it.

You are in danger and must leave Greece right away. I wish I could tell you in person, but I fear our meeting would only hasten the peril. I know you have no reason to heed my words, but please believe me. I lost you once, and could not bear to see it happen again if I can do anything to prevent it.

I am Julian Kostopoulos, born 1933 to Sara Kostopoulos, an extraordinary woman of many lives. It was the day of your 27th birthday and my 8th. Our birthday was one of many things we shared. You told me your secret as you lay dying in my arms. You made me swear that if we were to ever meet again, that I would tell you to leave Greece as quickly as possible. I had convinced myself over the years that my memory was nothing more than

wishful thinking of a young boy, longing to see his
mother again. When I saw you today, I knew it was
all true, and that I must not fail to carry out your
last request. Please leave tonight. I have enclosed a
key. You gave it to my father long ago for safe keep-
ing, and he gave to it me upon his passing. I wish I
could tell you what secret it unlocks. Please be safe. I
love you, mi̱ téra.
Always your loving son,
Julian

The last line of his letter hit me like a punch to the gut. *I love you, mi̱ téra. I love you, mama.* I could hear his voice saying it in my head, but not the voice of an elderly man. It was the sweet singsong voice of an eight-year-old boy; my eight-year-old boy. My son, Julian.

My hands trembled as I set the letter down on the nightstand. I was still wearing only a bathrobe, and a chill set through my body. I looked in the envelope, and inside was a small gold key. I shook the envelope, and the key dropped into the palm of my hand. I looked up at Luke. He was staring out the hotel window, almost motionless. He had read the letter already. I doubted this was the honeymoon he imagined when we booked the trip to Greece. Instead of a view of the Acropolis over cocktails, we were receiving a message from the past, an ominous warning that left us both at a loss for words.

"I'll start packing," he finally said, and walked away from the window without even looking in my direction.

"What? What do you mean? We can't leave now. I need to find out more from Julian. How can you even think about leaving now?" I asked, my voice more raised than I wanted.

"You read the same letter as I did. How can you think about staying? He said you are in danger. I haven't waited all these years to lose you now. We are leaving. Period," he replied.

I took a moment before I responded, not sure how to explain to Luke the deep need I felt to see Julian again. I didn't have my memories from my life as Sara Kostopoulos, not yet anyway, but I could feel Julian was my son. I couldn't leave him again, especially after the tragedy of his childhood.

"You can leave if you want to, but I'm staying. Whatever danger there may have been when I gave Julian that message has probably long since passed. Besides, how will I ever know what to do with this key if I don't find out more? Julian is the only lead we have," I said, hoping to convince to him to stay with me.

He sighed deeply. Twice. Then Luke looked at me and said, "I'll never leave you. No matter how bad I think this idea is, let's go find Julian. I don't know where this will lead us, but I'll be by your side the whole way."

CHAPTER 29

THE BEGINNING

It was a chilly morning. We loaded our luggage into the rental car for the drive to Nafplio, a small seaport town in the Peloponnese region of Greece. We managed to track down Julian's last known address, up the hillside near the north end of the Argolic Gulf. I didn't know what we would find, but I was grateful Luke would be at my side when we did. I knew he must be thinking about Julian's father. Up until now, I didn't think I had ever been in love before Luke. I had expected to remember more about that life by now, but it was still a distant blur. I couldn't remember anything about Julian's father; not his name, what he looked like, how we met, or if we had been in love. I thought back to just the day before, when Luke and I had landed in Athens to begin our honeymoon. It seemed like I finally had my happily-ever-after, but now the future was unclear; filled with more questions than answers. All I knew for sure was I had to see Julian again.

Luke started the car, and we began our journey to Nafplio. I fiddled with the map, completely lost without Siri to give me directions.

"Are you getting any signal yet?" I asked Luke. "I am not having much luck with this map."

"All those lives, and you didn't learn how to navigate with a map?" he asked. It was hard to tell if he was kidding or irritated. I imagined it was a bit of both.

"I guess the universe thought it more important I learn to knit," I replied.

Luke laughed, and for the first time that day, we relaxed enough to enjoy the beautiful scenery on our quest to find Julian. The entire area was filled with the lovely buildings and cottages, sprawling up from the beaches to the hilltop peaks. Looking out to the ocean, we saw Bourtzi Castle rising up from the brilliant blue waves. The impressive structure had played many roles in its long history, ranging from prison to luxury hotel and restaurant centuries later. Now it served as a brief distraction from the matter at hand, finding Julian and ultimately finding answers.

We allowed ourselves an hour to enjoy the view before moving on to the address given to us by the concierge at our hotel, who knew the name *Julian Kostopoulos* as soon as we asked. It was a short drive to his house on the hillside, and soon I was standing on the step of his front door.

"What are you waiting for?" Luke said, as anxious as I was.

I took three deep breaths, and rang the bell. It was the longest four minutes of my life; waiting for my 85-year-old son to come to the door. I finally heard his steps nearing, and then a pause as he looked out a small window to see who was at his home. The door opened slowly at first, but then there he was. My son, carefully leaning on a cane to steady himself, took a deep breath and invited me in.

"Please, come in *mi téra*. I hoped you would have taken my warning to heart and left Greece by now, but yet it makes my heart happy to see you," he said, inviting us inside.

"Julian, I am so sorry, for so many things. I never should have burdened you as such a young boy with such an ominous request. I'm sorry I couldn't follow your warning yesterday. I couldn't leave Greece without seeing you again. I need answers Julian. Anything you can tell me," I pleaded.

"Of course, *mi téra*," he said. "I will tell you everything you told me so long ago, and help you in any way I can. My heart is so full at this moment seeing you. Please come sit. We have much to discuss."

Then, for the first time in 77 years, I wrapped my arms around my son, and held him tight. "In a moment, my sweet boy. In a moment."

ABOUT THE AUTHOR

AMY LARSON MARBLE is a mom of four kids, a lawyer, and whose husband travels for work, so home-cooked meals or neatly made beds are a rarity. The family dogs Boomer, Finn, and Max (a.k.a. the pack) complete the chaos that is the daily routine. Amy was born in Colorado, grew up in North Dakota, and lives in Minnesota.

Years ago, Amy woke up after a dream of a girl who lived over and over again. That dream became the start of another dream, to write the story of Sarah and share it with others.

CPSIA information can be obtained
at www.ICGtesting.com
Printed in the USA
JSHW042054230520
5811JS00001B/22